Resurrection in a New World
The New World Book Five

Sherry Derr-Wille

Published by Rogue Phoenix Press, LLP
Copyright © 2022

ISBN: 978-1-62420-654-2

Credits
Cover Artist: Designs by Ms G
Editor: Amanda Armstrong

Dedication

To the producers of the *Ancient Aliens* TV presentation and all the contributors and researchers.

Chapter One

Diana Cruz applied her makeup carefully to cover the bruises she'd received days earlier at the hands of her husband, Stephen Cruz.

Thinking back on that night, she remembered putting the finishing touches to the evening meal. Stephen would be home soon and she wanted everything to be perfect. Earlier she'd insisted her teenage children eat an early supper and go to their rooms to do their homework.

Tonight, was special. It was their wedding anniversary. She'd planned the evening down to the last detail. As soon as he walked through the door, she lit the candles she'd placed on the table earlier in the afternoon.

"What the hell is all this shit about?" Stephen raged when he came in the door and saw the candle lit dining room.

"It's our anniversary, I made a special meal for us," she simpered, her words hardly louder than a soft whisper.

"Speak up, bitch."

She pulled herself together. "I said it's our anniversary. I…"

He cut her sentence short with a slap that sent her reeling.

"I don't smell any enchiladas. Are you so stupid that you don't know what day it is? We always have enchiladas on Tuesday. What in the hell were you thinking? You know I don't like all this fancy shit. I also like to see what I'm eating, so put out those stupid candles and turn on some lights so we can eat like civilized people."

Before she could douse the candles and turn on the lights, he attacked her, beating her about her face and upper body. With his rage depleted, he helped Diana to her feet.

"I guess I lost my temper. It's too late to make anything else, so we'll eat this slop that you prepared. I'll turn on the lights and blow out the candles while you serve me."

It took all of her energy to walk into the kitchen. As she picked up the silver tray she'd planned to use, she caught a glimpse of herself.

Bruises were already forming and blood trickled from her nose. At the sink she washed her face and staunched the flow of blood with cold compresses before she loaded the tray with green salads and assorted bottles of dressing. With the steaks cooking on the indoor grill, she took the salads into the dining room to serve Stephen.

An icy cold settled between them as they ate their salads. The alarm on the grill made her jump up from her chair to get the steaks and baked potatoes to bring to the table. She had no doubt the steaks would be done to a perfect medium rare, as the grill built into the stove always cooked food to perfection.

Once she set his steak in front of him, he tentatively cut into it as if expecting it to be either over or under cooked. He examined the piece of meat he'd speared with his fork. Even though she knew there was nothing to be concerned over, she cringed, half expecting to receive yet another beating.

At times like these she wondered why she put up with it, but she knew it was because she loved Stephen with all her heart. He was the father of her children and she had no desire to break up their family.

An alarm on her communicator alerted her to a message that was coming in. As soon as she tapped the screen, her husband's face came into view.

"Call my lawyer," he said, without giving her a proper greeting.

"Why?" she questioned.

"The cops just came and arrested me at my office. They gave me some trumped-up charges. Just do as I tell you, bitch." With that he ended the communication.

Panic set in as she frantically looked through Stephen's desk for the number for his lawyer. It took what seemed like hours, rather than the actual minutes it took for her to find the number and make connection with the lawyer.

"Stephen has been arrested," she told the lawyer.

"What are the charges?"

She sat quietly for a moment, as she realized she had no idea what her husband had been charged with. If he told her, she didn't remember.

"I don't know," she finally replied. "He just wanted me to call you. I'm sure you will figure it out once you get down to the station."

For the rest of the day, she worried about what was going on at the police station. The call didn't come through her communicator until just before the kids were due home from school. Even then it didn't come from Stephen but from his lawyer.

"I'm sorry to tell you this, but he's being charged with kidnapping, taking a minor across state lines and abuse. They are recommending he be held without bail until it's time for the trial."

Although Diana put on a brave face while talking to Stephen's lawyer, once he broke the connection, she allowed her tears to flow freely. Somehow, she was going to have to tell her kids what happened today. She knew it would change all of their lives forever.

Chapter Two

Diana, along with her children, sat in the courtroom to await the beginning of Stephen's trial. Over the past weeks, she'd only been allowed to visit him three times. The remainder of the lonely hours were spent holding not only her family and household together but keeping herself grounded without Stephen to lean on.

Diana sat on the side of the courtroom directly behind where Steven would be seated throughout the trial. Through her tears she watched as a young man, flanked by one of the aliens who seemed to be everywhere these days, entered the room. They seated themselves on the side of the room designated for prosecution witnesses.

Before she could concentrate on the young man and his companion, she saw her husband enter the room.

"Stephen, I love you. I know you're not guilty of what they're charging you with," she blurted out, knowing these were the words her husband expected her to say.

"Who is she?"

Although the words were whispered, Diana heard them and strained to hear how the alien would answer.

"She's your father's wife. The two kids sitting next to her are your half-brother and sister."

Diana could feel her stomach churn. Stephen Junior was his first-born son. He told her that when Stephen Junior was born. How dare this stranger profess to being her husband's son?

The prosecutor gave his opening statement, detailing how Stephen kidnapped Constance Montenegro from her loving family, abusing her and leaving her in the custody of his father when he was incarcerated for beating her.

Diana wished she could see the expression on Stephen's face, but of course that was impossible. She knew he must be appalled at the ludicrous accusations being levied against him.

When the prosecutor finished, the defense attorney made his opening statement, saying Constance Montenegro left her home willingly to be with him and he'd been railroaded when he was sent to prison for beating her. They'd engaged in an argument and she'd blown everything out of proportion.

The fact her husband had been in prison for beating this woman, whoever she might be, came as a shock. She knew it shocked her children as well.

A good-looking man, named Phillipe Montenegro, was the first person to take the stand.

"How do you know the defendant, Mr. Montenegro?" the prosecutor asked.

"We were in the same class in high school. I thought we were good friends, until he met my sister. He filled her head with a lot of nonsense about how they were in love. She wanted to quit school, but our father wouldn't allow it. The next night she and Stephen went on a date, but Connie never came home."

"By Connie, do you mean Constance Montenegro?"

"Yes, sir. At home we called her Connie. She was only sixteen and until the day he died, our father cursed the name of Stephen Cruz. He was positive Stephen kidnapped her and took her away. It wasn't until recently we learned what actually happened to our sister."

"How did you learn that?"

"We were watching the proceedings for the trial for the people who ran Henderson Ranch. One of the young men who testified was Mark Almanor. Afterward, we contacted a man by the name of Cassion, who has mentored Mark. He told us the boy was Connie's son. When we met him and compared DNA, we found he was our long-lost nephew."

"I have no more questions for this witness."

The testimony this man gave came as a complete surprise to Diana. If he had kidnapped and beaten this woman, it was entirely possible the young man sitting across from her could be her step-son.

Once the prosecutor took his seat, the defense attorney got to his feet in order to cross examine the witness.

"Mr. Montenegro, if the boy you met and claim as your nephew is Mark Almanor, how can you possibly be accusing my client of kidnapping your sister. Why aren't you looking for someone by the name of Almanor?"

"My sister was terrified of both your client and his father. After suffering a beating at the hands of Michael Cruz, she moved to Nevada and changed her name to Tessa Almanor. She also changed her son's name from Paco to Marco. Before she could make her way home to her family, she died from internal bleeding."

"That's irrelevant in this proceeding. My client isn't charged with murder."

"He should be. He must have known what his father was capable of doing. My sister was a minor, he stole her away from her family and took her across state lines. That in itself is a crime. I don't know what went on between the two of them. Maybe she thought she loved him and was going willingly. I would give anything to have been able to save her as well as her son."

Stephen suddenly got to his feet. "You lying bastard. Connie and I were in love. We did nothing wrong."

The judge banged his gavel, and the defense attorney forced Stephen to sit back down at the defendant's table.

How can Stephen say he loved this woman? He told me I was the only woman he ever loved. Was I a fool to believe him?

There were no more questions for the witness and he was allowed to leave the stand.

Jonathan Montenegro was the next to take the stand. His testimony mirrored that of his brother's, almost word for word.

Once his testimony was finished, the judge ordered a recess for the midday meal. As they were leaving the courtroom, Diana approached the young man as well as his uncles and the alien who intimidated her.

"Why are you doing this to my husband?" she asked. "He's a good man. We have two children together?"

"May I ask what your name is?" the young man, who wanted

everyone to believe he was Stephen's son, asked.

"I don't see why not, because I'll be testifying for the defense this afternoon. I'm Diana Cruz and these are my children, Stephen Junior and Theresa. I take it you're the little bastard who is trying to say Stephen is your father."

"I am a bastard only because my father never married my mother. He is my father and that makes you my step-mother and your children my half siblings. It seems like I find more family every time I turn around."

"You are no family to us. Once this fiasco is over, I will thank you to never contact any of us ever again." With that, she turned on her heel and walked in the opposite direction.

After having their midday meal, everyone returned to the courtroom for the afternoon of testimony.

The young man she confronted earlier was the first person called to the stand.

"Please state your name."

"My given name was Paco Montenegro but I have since changed it legally to Mark Almanor."

"Why have you changed your name?"

"I was four years old when my mother and I ran away from the bad man. I have later learned he was my paternal grandfather, Michael Cruz. My mother had taken a terrible beating and I was also hit. When he left the house, my mother stole money from his safe and we ran away. She told me we couldn't let anyone know who we were. She called me Marco."

Before the next question could be asked, Diana thought about her father-in-law. She had no doubt he could be a brutal man. Considering the way Stephen reacted when his temper boiled over or he'd had too much to drink, it was only natural to believe it was something he was used to seeing growing up in his father's home. It was possible he'd been an abused child.

"Why are you calling yourself Mark?"

The prosecutor's question brought her attention back to the trial she was witnessing.

"Marco was a frightened child who was all alone in his life. Mark is an adult name."

"What do you remember of your father?"

"Very little. I was three when he went away. My mother said he went away because he hurt her."

The defense attorney went on the attack as Mark finished his testimony.

"How do you know my client is your father?" he asked.

"My mother said he was and the bad man said his name when he was hurting my mother."

Mark began to cry and shake uncontrollably as he seemed to revert to his four-year-old self.

Hearing the distress in the young man's voice and watching his breakdown softened Diana's heart. What had he suffered because of her father-in-law? She didn't want to even think about it. Over the years Michael Cruz had been a loving grandfather to her children, even though over the past weeks since Stephen's arrest he'd often threatened her regarding her testimony and both trials.

The defense attorney said he had no more questions and Mark was allowed to leave the stand.

As soon as he stood to leave the stand, she saw his legs buckle. In no time, the alien and his two uncles were at his side.

"Are you all right, young man?" the judge asked.

"He will be," the alien replied. "Because of this man and his father, Mark has lived through a very traumatic childhood."

"Just who are you?" the judge questioned.

"I am Cassion, from the Council of Intergalactic Affairs. I am a lawyer who is here to represent Mark's interests. He needs to rest. I will take him back to the complex…"

"No," Mark interrupted. "I want to see this through. I'll be fine."

Even though the young man appeared weak, she marveled at his determination to stay in the courtroom for the remainder of the trial.

"Then we'll continue," the judge replied.

"The prosecution rests, your honor," the prosecutor proclaimed.

The defense attorney called Diana. "Please state your name."

"My name is Diana Cruz. Stephen Cruz is my husband."

"What do you know of the charges brought against Stephen Cruz?"

"I know these are trumped-up charges. My husband is the gentlest man in the world." She knew it was a lie, but she understood it was the testimony Stephen wanted her to give. "He doesn't have a mean bone in his body. He could have never done the things you are accusing him."

"Do you know anything about the woman he's accused of kidnapping, Constance Montenegro?"

"I've never heard her name until all of this came about. As for the bastard who says he is Stephen's son, he's a liar. The only children Stephen has are mine, Stephen Junior and Theresa."

The prosecuting attorney had no questions for Diana. Since she was merely a character witness, she was relieved not to have to endure a brutal cross-examination.

The next witness was Stephen. After stating his name, he took a seat in the witness box.

"Do you know Constance Montenegro?" his attorney asked.

"We dated in high school. When her father wouldn't let us get married, we ran away together. Later she lied to the police and said I beat her. I ended up going to prison because of that bitch."

"Did you have a child with Constance?"

"Yes, I did. His name was Paco, but the bitch wouldn't give him my last name. She was pissed off because I hadn't married her. He could have been anyone's brat. I wasn't around long enough to know if he was mine or not."

"Did you have him DNA chipped?"

"Hell no. That's just a way for the government to keep track of you. She had him at home so that we didn't have to pay a doctor to deliver him or pay to have him chipped."

"Were you aware she was a minor when you took her across state lines?"

"She told me she was eighteen and now I know she lied. When I mentioned that she was two years behind me in school, she said it was because she was stupid and failed two years."

"Do you know what happened to her when you were in prison?"

"My father said he'd take care of her and her brat, even if it wasn't mine."

The prosecutor got to his feet. "Were you or were you not a friend of Phillipe Montenegro?"

"We were in the same class in school, but that doesn't mean we were exactly friends. I knew she was his sister. When she told me she was eighteen, I figured they were probably twins. It was believable that she got the short end of the stick in the brains department. That didn't matter much to me. She was good in bed, even though I figured she was spreading her legs for several of my friends."

Before anyone could stop him, Mark was on his feet. "Liar," he shouted.

His action shocked Diana, as well as most of the other people in the courtroom.

"Do you have a DNA chip, Mr. Cruz?" the prosecutor questioned

"What the hell for?"

"To compare it with Mr. Almanor."

"Yes, I have one, but I'm positive that bastard isn't mine."

The judge looked over at Stephen. "I call for a brief recess so our medical personnel can scan your chip as well as that of Mr. Almanor."

"When did the little bastard get chipped?"

The alien got to his feet. "If I may, your honor, I would like to answer the defendant's question."

"You may. Please step forward and be sworn in."

Diana watched as Stephen was led back to the defendant's table where medical personnel were ready to read his DNA chip.

"Do you know when Mr. Almanor was chipped?"

"I do. He was orphaned when his mother died and with no identification, he was sent to Henderson Ranch. At the age of eighteen, he aged out of the program and was sold as a slave to a ranch in Mexico. We rescued him when we learned of what was going on at that ranch. By the time we got him to our facility in Denver, we knew nothing of his background. It was at that time his DNA was tested and a chip was implanted. Through that chip we were able to find the brothers of his mother and learn more of what transpired before and after he was born."

She watched as Mark sat quietly listening when the medical personnel came to read his chip. It was a painless process, everyone knew that, but the way his father acted when he had it done, she was worried about the results. She prayed what Stephen said on the stand would prove to be true and the boy belonged to one of his friends. It was easier to think of the woman as a whore than to believe what her husband was being charged with.

The alien, who stated his name as Cassion, returned to his seat as the doctor took the stand.

"What were your findings?' the judge asked.

"The scan shows that Mr. Cruz and Mr. Almanor are father and son."

"The court thanks you."

Diana could feel the color drain from her face as though the blood had suddenly left her body. To her surprise, Stephen Junior got to his feet.

"I'd like to testify," her son said.

"You can't," Stephen protested. "You're too young."

For the first time since this nightmare began, she agreed with her husband. Even though she'd allowed her son and daughter to attend the trial, she didn't want him scared by having to testify.

"I'd like to hear what this young man has to say," the judge declared. "You may take the stand, son."

Stephen Junior walked past his father, with his head held high. At that moment, she was so proud of him, she thought her heart would burst.

"Can you state your name and age?"

"My name is Stephen Cruz Junior. I'm fifteen."

"What did you want to tell the court?"

"My mother lied when she was on the stand. She said what my father told her to say. If she told the truth and he got to come home, she was afraid he would beat her again."

Diana's gasp was audible. Although her son told the truth, he'd actually called her a liar.

"Have you witnessed this abuse?"

"Many times. He's even started beating on me. I was afraid he was going to start hitting my sister. I don't want that to happen."

Shock was the only way for her to respond to her son's testimony. She had no idea of the abuse her husband was piling on him. Had she known, would she have been able to stop it?

"Did you know about your half-brother?"

"Not until today, but I'd like to know more about him."

"Thank you for your honesty, son. You can return to your seat."

Rather than looking directly at her, Stephen Junior turned his gaze to Mark. She wondered if he was in awe of his older half-brother. Could she, in all honesty, keep them from becoming acquainted in the near future?

The judge recalled Diana to the stand. Once there, she had no recourse but to recant her earlier testimony stating that her husband threatened her with further bodily harm if she told the truth. As she did, she remembered visiting with him at the jail and him telling her what she was to say at his trial. She also recalled the night of their sixteenth wedding anniversary when he beat her because she didn't serve the enchiladas as was their custom for that night of the week.

How could I have been such a fool? she asked herself as she returned to her seat.

Both attorneys made closing arguments and the jury was dismissed.

As they got up to leave the courtroom, Stephen Junior walked over to where Mark was standing. She followed his lead with Theresa by her side.

"After today, I guess we're brothers. Are you going to be staying in Arizona?"

She watched as Mark shook her son's hand. "No, I'm getting my schooling in Denver and will be moving to Nevada where I've been offered a job as a ranch manager. Once I'm there, I'll be studying to be a veterinarian."

"Will I ever see you again and get to know you?"

"Once I'm on the ranch, it's possible you could come and spend some time there."

"I hope so. I've always wanted a big brother."

"Whatever, I think you should clear it with your mother. I don't think she would be too happy with you coming to the ranch. Don't do anything to cause her any more anguish than she's going through."

Mark's words meant the world to Diana. She was certain Stephen Junior would want someone to look up to if things went badly for his father. The young man's concern for her wellbeing meant the world and all to her.

"I understand. I'm sure Theresa will want to get to know you as well. Of course, we won't do anything without Mother's approval."

Although Diana had been monitoring their conversation from a safe distance, she moved closer to the two young men, one her son and the other her step-son.

"I'm sorry, Mark," she said. "I can't imagine what your life has been like. I lied because Stephen and his father both threatened me. That was foolish. Can you forgive me?"

"I've been learning about the One God and forgiveness. I can forgive you because He has saved me. I hope we can be friends, and I can get to know Stephen Junior and Theresa."

They were ready to leave the courthouse when the clerk came out to tell them the jury was back with the verdict.

Diana's nerves kicked in as she took her seat across from Mark. Whether or not the jury found Stephen Cruz guilty, there could be repercussions and retaliation against her family because of the accusations. If the retaliation came from Stephen or their friends, the result would be the same. She didn't know if she or her children could survive either way.

When asked about the verdict, the foreperson said they were all in agreement. When the judge nodded, the foreperson read the verdict. "On the charge of kidnapping, we find the defendant guilty. On the charge of taking a minor across state lines, we find the defendant guilty."

Diana's shoulders slumped in relief. She had no idea she'd been holding her breath until she felt the tension begin to leave her body.

"Stephen Cruz, you have been found guilty of all charges. You are hereby sentenced to life in prison in the state penitentiary, with no chance for parole."

By the time Stephen was led out of the courtroom, he ranted and raved about the unfairness of his sentence.

Diana remained seated until the courtroom emptied. Throughout this trial, she'd been so focused, she didn't think about returning less than twenty-four hours later for the trial of her father-in-law, Michael Cruz, for the murder of Mark's mother.

As she had with Stephen, she'd been in denial of the possibility of either of them being convicted of the charges against them. Now she wasn't so certain. Even though Michael used threats to get her to lie for Stephen, she was skeptical of the charges of murder being leveled against her father-in-law. The revelations of today's trial shone a whole new light on the situation.

Chapter Three

The courtroom was packed when Diana saw Mark and the others in his party arrive. It pleased her when Mark acknowledged them with a nod of his head. Earlier, Stephen Junior indicated he wanted to talk to his half-brother. She knew he wanted her blessing and she gladly gave it. She didn't have to strain to be able to eavesdrop on their conversation.

"My family wants to get to know you better," Stephen said. "We talked about things last night and my mother has decided to have our last name changed to her maiden name of Alverez. I also made the decision to go by my nickname of Buck. Theresa also wants to be called Terri. We want nothing to do with the man who fathered us."

"You've made a good decision, just as I did when Cassion helped me to have my name changed legally."

"We've been doing some research, especially after what you said about taking over Resurrection Ranch. Mom wants to know if there would be a place for us there? She's a trained teacher as well as a good cook. We want to be included in your project."

She could tell Mark was taken by surprise with their offer.

"I don't know, Buck. All of this is in the planning stage. What about your educations? You and Terri deserve more out of life than living on a cattle ranch."

It was Cassion who joined them. "I couldn't help overhearing your conversation. I have been working behind the scenes, so to say, to get Mark's project off the ground. Since we are planning to have an educational facility on the property, I am certain your mother would be a welcome addition to the staff. From what I've been told, there is a house on the property that is being rehabbed. It might take us a few months, but I'm positive something can be worked out. Mark deserves to have the family he's been denied for his entire life."

Steven, now called Buck, took his seat next to his mother.

"I'm so proud of you," she said, squeezing his hand. "You only forgot one thing. From now on I plan to be called Diane. Like Mark said, this is my grown-up name. I feel like I'm ready to begin our new lives."

"Do you think they will let us move there?" Terri asked.

"I'm sure they will. I think the One God is orchestrating things here on earth."

The bailiff announced that court was in session and everyone should take their seats, ending their conversation.

The prosecutor laid out his case of how Michael Cruz had taken custody of Constance Montenegro and her son, when his son, Stephen, had been sent to prison. Because of his cruelty, Constance was forced to flee his home after he had severely beaten her, causing her untimely death.

The first witness was a man named Jason Culver.

"How did you come to know of Constance Montenegro, Officer Culver?"

"I was on patrol in Elko, Nevada. It was at the end of my shift around four thirty in the morning, when I saw a young boy alone on the sidewalk. He told me his mother wouldn't wake up and he was hungry. When I asked him where he lived, he directed me to an apartment building, not far from where he was standing."

"What did you find in the apartment building?"

"I found an apartment door open. When I went in the rooms were very neat. As I walked through, I entered a bedroom and found a young woman lying on the bed. I tried to wake her, but her body was cold to the touch. It was evident she was dead and had been for several hours. As we did more investigation, we learned the name on the lease she'd signed for the apartment was Tessa Almanor and she was living there with her son, Marco. That was the name the little boy gave me when I found him on the sidewalk."

"What did you learn was the cause of her death?"

"The medical examiner who did the autopsy, told me Tessa died a slow and painful death from a beating she'd taken. He said there were several ruptured internal organs and she slowly bled to death. It was enough to make me sick to my stomach."

"What happened to the child?"

Jason looked directly at Mark before he continued his testimony. Diane did the same thing, wondering how this would affect Mark.

"Since he had no family that we could find, he was sent to Henderson Ranch. At the time, I thought it was going to be the perfect place for him. I'd heard how they were funded by the state of Nevada and took in orphans to raise them. It wasn't until recently that the world learned he'd been sent to hell on earth."

"How did you come to equate Tessa Almanor with Constance Montenegro?"

"It wasn't until I attended the trial for the Hendersons and met Mark Almanor and his uncles Phillip and Jonathan Montenegro. That was when I remembered a missing person report I'd received about a month after finding Tessa and Marco. It was put out by Michael Cruz and he was looking for Constance Montenegro and her son Paco. At that time, everything seemed to fall into place. I talked to Mark and he confirmed that his name had been Paco, but his mother told him never to tell it to everyone because the 'bad man' would find them. It didn't take long for me to realize the 'bad man' was Michael Cruz."

As much as the defense attorney tried to shake Jason's story, he could not be swayed to change his testimony.

The next person to take the stand was Anna Manning.

Diane wasn't surprised, as she'd been contacted by Anna the evening before. She'd told her that, had she still been married to Michael, she would be grandmother to Buck and Tessa as well as Diane's mother-in-law. Seeing her in person, she was amazed at the fact she was a small woman. She was hardly a match for Michael Cruz.

"How do you know Michael Cruz?" the prosecutor asked her.

"We were married for six years. After I gave birth to our son, Stephen, I thought we had the perfect marriage. By the time Stephen was four years old, Michael changed. He started abusing me, mentally, sexually and physically. I told him I was leaving and taking Stephen with me. He told me if I took his son away from him, he would kill me to get him back. He made me promise I would leave my child and never go to the police, in order to save my life. Over the years I have often wondered what happened to my former husband and my child. Little did I know they had moved to the Phoenix area, just a few miles from my home in Mesa."

"Did you divorce Michael?"

"I did, but my lawyer could never find him. They were looking for him in Nebraska where we were living at the time of our marriage. I have since met a wonderful man and have an entirely new family and identity. How anyone found me to testify at this trial is beyond my comprehension."

The prosecutor ended his questioning and was replaced by the defense attorney.

"You testified that you abandoned your four-year-old child. Is that correct?"

"I told my husband I wanted to leave with our son, but he wouldn't allow it. I was lucky to have escaped with my life. I prayed my husband had not abused our son in the same way he did me."

"Yes, but you abandoned your son. Doesn't that make you an unfit mother?"

"I was not an unfit mother. I was a young woman in fear of losing her life. The only way I could escape was to leave my child. Had I stayed, Michael would have killed me. Had I taken my son with me, he would have killed me to get our son back. I left to protect myself as well as my son. Without me, I was certain he wouldn't kill our son."

The attorney kept badgering Anna until the prosecutor finally objected to his method of questioning. Once the judge made a decision about the line of questioning, Anna was excused.

Diane marveled at how composed Anna remained under the questioning of the defense attorney. No matter what the circumstances of their meeting, she knew she and Anna would become close friends.

Finally, it was Mark's turn to take the stand. Diana wondered what he could testify to, especially sixteen years after the events that took his mother's life.

Again, Mark stated his name as well as his age.

"How do you know the defendant, Michael Cruz?" the prosecutor asked.

"I never knew his name. What do names mean when you're three and four years old? I remember he wanted me to call him Grandfather and later Papa. I only thought of him as the bad man."

"Did you ever see your grandfather strike your mother?"

Diana saw the small child in Mark threatening to return. "More than once."

"Did he ever hit you?"

Mark nodded his head as though the words seemed to be stuck in his throat.

"Please Mr. Almanor, you must answer verbally."

He swallowed hard. "Yes, he did. The last time was the night my mother and I ran away from him. He was beating my mother and I yelled at him to leave my mother alone. He turned on me and hit me so hard I flew across the room. When I stood up, blood was running down my lip. I was afraid he was going to kill me."

He answered a few more questions before the defense attorney began his cross examination.

"You tell quite a story, young man. With children's memories, it's hard to tell fact from fiction. You called my client the bad man. Wasn't that like when children are afraid of the boogie man under the bed. Isn't this all a figment of a child's over active imagination?"

Mark appeared to be appalled, but seemed determined to hold his temper in check.

"I've made up nothing. I've relived the life we endured every night in my nightmares. It wasn't until recently that I was able to put a name to the bad man from my past."

"You testified that you and your mother left your grandfather's house. Can you tell me about how your mother stole money from your grandfather?"

"It was the night he beat my mother for the last time and made my nose bleed. My mother told me she took money from Grandfather's safe so we could run away and start a new life."

"Was that when she changed your name?"

"Yes, it was. She told me I should never tell anyone my real name was Paco and from now on I would be Marco. I thought it was a strange game, but I was happy that we wouldn't have to be hurt by the 'bad man' any longer."

"Do you realize your mother was a criminal?"

"My mother was a good woman. She only took the money so we could get away from him." Mark got to his feet and pointed his finger directly at his grandfather.

The courtroom erupted in gasps of amazement, causing the judge to bang his gavel on his desk, ordering everyone to be quiet.

She watched as Mark sat back down and appeared to take a deep breath to calm himself.

"Are you okay to continue, Mr. Almanor?" the judge asked.

Diane was horrified when rather than answering the judge's question, Mark pitched forward in a dead faint. Almost immediately the two men who yesterday had identified themselves as Mark's uncles were at his side, helping him to the floor from the witness box.

All around them the courtroom was abuzz at the turn of events. Amid the chaos, the judge was pounding his gavel and calling for order.

Almost immediately, Diane heard sirens. Someone must have called for assistance. It was the alien who explained the situation to the paramedics.

"Here, eat this," she heard one of the uncles say.

Whatever he gave Mark, it worked like magic. The dull look in his eyes disappeared and color began to return to his cheeks.

"We need to check you over, Sir," the lead paramedic said. "We've been apprised of your condition, but we would like to make certain your vitals are returning to normal."

Diane was relieved when Mark nodded his head in approval. It was always better to be safe than sorry.

After the paramedics took his vitals and were satisfied that he was in no immediate danger, he allowed his uncles to help him to his feet.

Once he was again seated, it came as a surprise when Cassion was called to the stand to testify.

"Cassion, you have testified that you are one of the aliens from the Denver Complex. What is your connection to this case?"

Diane listened as Cassion detailed how Chris had come to the complex after being rescued from the militant group. With his rescue, Cassion said it became a mission of his to find other survivors of Henderson Ranch.

"When Mr. Almanor was brought to your complex, what was his condition?"

"He was suffering with malnutrition and dehydration. What happened here today is a side effect of what he was suffering from. He was treated last night after the trial for his father yesterday. He has been abused for his entire life and is only now coming to grips with the ramifications of what has been done to him."

Hearing what Mark's life had been like brought tears to Diane's eyes. Motherly instincts kicked in and she wanted nothing more than to take him into her arms and comfort him.

The judge announced they would be adjourning for lunch. As Diane left the room, it was Anna who came to her side immediately.

"I didn't know if you would be here today, even though you said you would," Anna began. "I'm so glad you came. I want to get to know not only you, but also my grandchildren."

"I've been anxious to get to know you as well," Diane said.

"Grandfather always told us you were dead," Buck began. "I'm glad you aren't dead. I'm thrilled to have another grandmother in my life."

Anna thanked them profusely and turned her attention to Mark, who was coming out of the courtroom with his uncles and Cassion. For some reason, Diane decided to follow Anna as she approached Mark and the others.

"I realize this must be overwhelming for you," Anna said. "I just want to tell you how proud you make me. I've regretted leaving your father with my ex-husband all my life, but I knew taking him away would have been a death sentence for both of us. From what I've learned today, perhaps I should have allowed Michael to kill the both of us."

Her statement overwhelmed Diane. It was unthinkable that Anna would say such a thing.

It was Mark who answered her statement. "If he'd killed you and my father, I would not be here. I have a feeling the One God has a purpose for me and it doesn't include never being born. I want to get to know you and I'm certain we will be getting together in the future. For now, though, I need to take care of myself and make a workable plan for the future."

"I can understand that. All I ask is that you don't forget me." With that, she backed away and returned to where Diane and her family were standing.

~ * ~

If Diane thought she'd seen the last of her husband, she was sadly mistaken. The first witness for the defense was Stephen Cruz. He was brought into the courtroom wearing an orange jumpsuit and his hands were electronically shackled.

After he was sworn in, he took the witness stand.

"How do you know the defendant?" the defense attorney asked.

"He's my dad."

"What about Constance Montenegro? How do you know her?"

"She lied about her age and encouraged me to run away with her. We lived together and had a son, Paco, but she kept nagging about getting married. One night we were having an argument and she called the cops on me. The bitch was very convincing and I got sent away to prison."

"What became of Constance and Paco?"

"My father took them into his house, out of the goodness of his heart. Neither of us were happy about her not giving our son my last name. Even so, he looked after her and the brat until the night she took money out of his safe and disappeared. We didn't know if they were dead or alive, but since we were never married, I found love with another woman and built a real family."

Diane thought she was going to be sick. It was evident that Stephen never loved her. If he had, he would never beaten her in the way he did on several occasions.

"What about the accusations that your father beat not only her but also your son?"

"She was a conniving little bitch. I'm certain she told people a very convincing story. I have no doubts that she's dead, but it was probably because she was using drugs and overdosed. I wouldn't put anything past her. The people who are trying to pin a murder that might or might not have happened sixteen years ago on my father are lying just like she did."

The smile on the face of the defense attorney said he thought the jury would believe every word that came out of Stephen's mouth.

The prosecuting attorney got to his feet and walked across the room to stand in front of the witness box. "I have the autopsy report for Constance Montenegro. It states that she died of internal injuries as well as bleeding from those injuries caused by a beating. There were no drugs in her system. What do you have to say about that?"

"Cops are cops, no matter where they are. They've had it in for my family for years. I'm certain they were more than happy to have the report doctored to suit their purposes."

"Until recently no one knew that Constance Montenegro and Tessa Almanor were one and the same. That being the case, why would anyone have a reason to doctor the report for Tessa Almanor?"

The expression on Stephen's face was one of shock. Everything he'd testified to was being destroyed by the evidence in the autopsy report.

When Stephen was excused, an officer came and led him away. It was possible he was being held in a facility in Phoenix before he, and hopefully his father, would be transferred to the state prison.

It came as no surprise that Michael didn't take the stand. Even though he was a smooth talker, it was possible the cross examination would denounce everything he testified to.

With no further witnesses, the attorneys gave their closing arguments and the jury left to come to their decision about guilt or innocence.

Like the jury the day before, the verdict was reached within an hour of the start of deliberations. The results were guilty of murder in the second degree.

"Michael Cruz, you have been found guilty of murder in the second degree," the judge said. "I wish we could have proved that the murder of Constance Montenegro was premeditated so I could sentence you to death. Of course, we know the death penalty has been abolished. Since that is not the case, I sentence you to life imprisonment at the state penitentiary with no chance for parole."

Before Michael could be shackled and taken out of the court room, he turned to face Mark. "This is your fault, you little bastard. If your mother hadn't been such a lying little bitch who stole money from me, none of this would have ever happened. It's too bad I didn't kill her and you on the night she ran away and stole my money. I hope you burn in hell for what you've done to me."

Her father-in-law's words were like a knife being stuck in her heart. To her relief, Mark refused to stoop to the old man's level. It would have been easy to lash out against him and repeat the vile words he'd spoken. The maturity of this young man was evident, even though he'd suffered unmentionable horrors because of his grandfather's actions.

Diane was surprised when Anna suggested they all meet for dinner that night. She assured Diane that Mark as well as his uncles and Cassion were also invited.

The restaurant Anna chose was one of the most elegant restaurants in Phoenix.

"Whether you like it or not," Anna said, once they were seated at the table and their orders were taken, "you are my family. Mark, you, Buck and Terri are my grandchildren. If things had been different, Diane, you would have been my daughter-in-law. I am not without means. In other words, my late husband left me very well off. Unfortunately, my children from my second marriage no longer live in the area. My son, David, is an architect in Dallas and my daughter, Cindy, is married to a doctor who works in Peru. That said, I want to get to know all of you better. I would be honored if you would allow me to invest some of the money in Resurrection Ranch and perhaps even relocate there."

It was evident Mark was at a loss for words.

It was Jonathan who replied to the offer. "I think we can all work together on this. My brother and I are both investing in Resurrection Ranch. Cassion has offered his help and several people from the Denver Complex are interested in coming there to work as well. What you need to know is there are several young men, like Mark and his friend, Chris, who have been deprived of an education and a family because of the Hendersons. They are also scarred by the way they ran the ranch for far too many years. To begin with, the ranch will be catering to educating them and giving them a secure future."

"I've done my homework. When I first read about my ex-husband being charged with murder, I didn't think it had anything to do with me. I was interested in what I was reading about my son, as well as the two families he had. I thought about the fact I had grandchildren I might never know. If I hadn't gotten the communication from the prosecuting attorney, I would have found a way to connect with all of you at a later date.

"For you, Mark, it breaks my heart to know how you were raised and the horrors you've survived. I want to make a difference in your life.

"That brings me to Buck and Terri. I have a feeling the two of you suffered more than any of us will ever know at the hands of your father. It pains me to think my son followed in the footsteps of his father. They are both cruel men and I pray that you two becoming involved with Resurrection Ranch will break the chain of brutality that has ruled this family for far too long."

"I didn't give you enough credit, Anna," Jonathan said. "It hasn't been that long since Phil and I were the ones asking Mark to accept us as family. At the time we doubted his connection to us, but the DNA proved he was definitely our nephew. Yesterday, your son also doubted Mark, but again the DNA brought about a revelation I'm sure he didn't want to accept. You are more accepting than any of us."

"All my life, I've wished I had a family," Mark finally said. "I don't remember much about my father, but I do remember my mother. I've always thought she was the only family I would ever have and she'd been taken away from me. Now suddenly, I have uncles, a grandmother, a step-mother as well as a half-brother and sister. You'll all have to bear with me, because this is something completely unknown to me. I don't know what to do with family."

Anna got up and came to where Mark was sitting. "You might not know what to do with us, but we know what to do with you. Let us into your world and let us love you."

Diane echoed Anna's words. Her children had immediately accepted Mark and now she wanted to show him a mother's love, even though he was an adult, learning to make his way in this new world.

Chapter Four

"What are your plans for the immediate future?" Anna asked as they were checking out of their hotel the following morning.

"I hardly know where to start," Diane admitted. "The children need to finish school for the year and prepare for the move out to Resurrection Ranch."

"It's definite then?"

"Cassion talked to me last night after dinner and said the main house should be ready for us by the end of this school year. That will give me time to liquidate our property. The court awarded Michael's assets for the children, so I'll have to liquidate that as well. I'm planning to split the proceeds three ways in order that Mark will get a share, even if he doesn't think he wants it. If nothing else we can invest it in the ranch."

"I was also contacted by the courts. They asked me if I would be able to help you with the liquidation. I told them I would have to think about it and I know you will want to think on it too."

"I agree. I'm so overwhelmed, I hardly know where to start, but I don't want to make any rash decisions."

"Cassion talked to me as well. He said the main house is large enough for me to join you there. What I want to know is if you will be comfortable sharing your accommodations with me?"

Diane laughed at Anna's question. "That is funny, considering last night the kids asked me if you could live with us on the ranch. At the time, we didn't know if you were even interested in moving there."

"Oh, my dear, I've thought of nothing else since I learned I have three grandchildren I never knew existed. There is nothing for me in Mesa, other than a house filled with memories of happier days with my husband. Like you, I will need to liquidate my assets and prepare for the move whenever I get the word, they are ready for me out there. I'm not a teacher, but I do love to garden and to cook. I think we would make one dynamic team."

Without reservation, Diane embraced Anna. It was, indeed, time for a new start for all of them. The publicity Stephen garnered, with not only his arrest but also his trial, had been hard on her children. It was no wonder they were so acceptable to changing their names.

~ * ~

The next morning, after the kids left for school, Diane contacted a lawyer, just not the one who represented Stephen at the trial.

Terrez Harper was recommended by one of her few friends who still had anything to do with her. With an appointment set for that afternoon, she left a note for the kids, before driving to Terrez's downtown office.

Although she thought she'd be nervous, she felt more confident than she ever had since she'd been married to Stephen. The building housing the office was one that had been erected in the early twenty-first century, or so it said on the plaque imbedded in the brick of the building. Inside, the décor reminded her of pictures she'd seen in the retro decorating magazines she enjoyed browsing through.

Terrez's office was on the fifth floor. After introducing herself to the secretary in the outer office, she waited to be called to go in and meet with her lawyer.

To her surprise, Terrez was definitely one of the aliens. Her tall stature combined with her violet eyes and bright white hair left no doubt.

"I'm pleased to have you choose me to represent your interests," Terrez said, extending her hand. "I must admit, I've been following the trials of your husband and father-in-law. Cassion is my uncle and it was good to get to see him while he was here. How did you hear about me?"

"You were recommended by my friend, Jana Passer."

"Oh yes, Jana. She was one of my first clients when I started my practice. She asked me to help her when she opened her boutique. We've socialized several times in the last couple of years. What can I help you with?"

"I need to liquidate the assets of my husband and my father-in-law. That will include both houses, a mountain cabin, all of the furnishings and my husband's business."

Terrez looked shocked. "If you're liquidating everything, where will you and your children live?"

"We're planning to relocate to Nevada and start new lives. I'd also like to have you handle my divorce from my husband as well as the official changing of our names. We are changing our last names to Alvarez. I'd like to change my first name from Diana to Diane, Stephen Junior's first name to Buck, and Theresa's first name to Terri."

Terrez nodded. "I can understand your need to distance yourself from the Cruz family. May I ask why you chose Alverez?"

"It's my maiden name. My son was the one who suggested it. He's been having some backlash about his father ever since he was arrested."

"You've got a very wise son. It's hard to believe he's only fifteen. You see, I did monitor the trial. I was impressed with him when he took the stand to testify against his father. It was very courageous of him."

It took over two hours for Diane to fill out all the papers necessary for the liquidation of the assets that suddenly became hers, to say nothing about the papers for legally changing their names.

By the time she got home, she was surprised to find that Buck, as he now wanted to be called, had already started preparing their evening meal.

"I got your note. I figured you'd be tired, so I got out hamburger patties and called the store to have the rest of our supper delivered. I hope you don't mind."

"Of course, I don't mind. I was wondering what I had in the cupboards. If I didn't have to go to the lawyer's office today, I should have gone grocery shopping."

She sat down her purse just as the automated system announced that she had a delivery from the local grocery store.

After tipping the delivery person, she assessed her son's purchases. Along with the pickles, onion, lettuce and tomatoes were an assortment of his favorite salads. Also in the bag was a package of hamburger buns.

When she entered the kitchen, she noticed that Terri had set the table with the good china, crystal, silverware and cloth napkins. It reminded her of the night of her wedding anniversary when she made a special meal for Stephen only to have him berate and beat her because it wasn't what he wanted to eat.

"Even if this is like an indoor picnic, I decided it should be an elegant affair. I've decided we should celebrate our freedom and our new lives."

Terri's statement brought tears to Diane's eyes. "I love the two of you so much. I am so sorry for everything that has been going on over the past few months."

"It wasn't your fault, Mom," Buck declared. "I should have said something about how he beat me but I knew what he was capable of doing. I didn't want him to hurt you because of me. I also didn't want him hurting Terri. We're so much better off without him."

Diane nodded. Terrez had been right when she said her son was a courageous young man.

After saying grace, they sat down to their fancy indoor picnic.

"How was your school day?" she asked, not certain she wanted to hear what her kids had to say.

She could tell by the looks on her children's' faces, things hadn't gone well for either of them.

"I wish we could move out to Resurrection Ranch right now," Buck declared. "Everyone avoided me like I had the plague. I talked to the counselor and she suggested I might want to finish the rest of the school year online. I told her we would be relocating after school let out for the summer and she said she thought it was a good idea. If it hadn't been for my friend, Julian, I would have got beaten up by some of the bullies. He was the one who rushed me to the counselor's office. When the counselor suggested the online option, he agreed. I guess he's been taking some flak for being my friend. He's going to transfer to online school as well. We'll be starting the classes online tomorrow."

Diane's heart ached for her son. Why were kids so cruel? "Are you sure this is what you want?" she finally asked.

"Positive. I've taken too many beatings from Dad. I don't want to repeat the experience in order to finish my year at school."

"I got the same offer from my counselor," Terri admitted. "Someone had spray-painted 'bitch' on my locker and a lot of kids made nasty comments about Dad and Grandpa. They said I was just as bad as them. Since I have my own laptop, as well as a communicator, they were able to load all of my classes onto them. I start tomorrow, just like Buck."

"I am so sorry about what your father and grandfather have put you through."

"It's not your fault, Mom," Terri said, consolingly.

"What was your day like, Mom?" Buck asked, between bites of his hamburger.

"I went to see the lawyer my friend, Jana, recommended. She is going to take care liquidating everything. This weekend, we have to decide what we want to take to Nevada with us and start packing. If the sale goes quickly, we'll have to put some things in storage and move into a rental property until the end of the school year."

"What about changing our names?" Terri inquired.

"She's taking care of that as well as my divorce from your father. It won't be long before we can begin our new lives."

"What about Grandma Anna? Do you think she will be able to help you with Grandpa's assets?" Buck questioned.

"I hope she says she will. That would take a lot of stress off my shoulders. No matter what she decides, it will have to be her decision."

Chapter Five

Without the worry of the liquidation of Stephen and Michael's assets, Diane felt a load lift from her shoulders. Even though she knew she didn't need to work, she went back to her office and started the process of closing up her professional life in Phoenix.

"What are you planning to do now?" her boss asked her, when they met for lunch.

"I'd like to continue working until the school year ends, if you'll have me. By that time, I should have all of my husband and his father's assets liquidated. I'm also changing our names. You will probably be advised of the change soon. I'm going back to my maiden name of Alverez and changing Diana to Diane. The kids are anxious to no longer be called by the last name of Cruz. They've both gone to online schooling because of the harassment of their fellow students. It's so hard on them. Last night they said they wished they could move to Resurrection Ranch right away. Of course, we all know that's not possible. I guess that's why this job is so important to me. Until things can be cleared up, I need to work to support the kids."

"Why wouldn't I want you to stay on? You're the best employee I have. I hate to see you go, but with what has been going on I don't blame you for getting out of Phoenix. Those trials were two of the biggest stories to hit Phoenix in years."

Diane was pleased to still have the confidence of her employer. It would make the next few weeks easier to endure.

Once they were back at work, her communicator indicated she had a message. Confident she wouldn't be hearing from Stephen, she answered without checking the identity of the sender.

"What do you think you're doing, bitch?" Stephen shouted. "How dare you divorce me? What's this about you liquidating not only my assets but also those that belong to my father?"

Diane took a deep breath. "When you and your father were convicted, the state confiscated all of your property. As your wife, everything was turned over to me. I'm doing what is necessary for our children's futures. About the divorce, did you think I could remain married to a man who will never be released from prison? Everything is for the best. Don't ever try to contact me again because I will be blocking you as soon as we finish this transmission."

She touched the button to end the communication and the screen went black. As she promised, she immediately blocked Stephen from contacting her in the future.

"I could hear Stephen shouting at you in my office," her boss said, coming to her desk. "Are you okay?"

"I am now. I thought I wouldn't be hearing from him again. To my surprise, I stayed calm and never shed a tear. He's where he should be and he can't hurt us any longer. When I get home tonight, I'll contact my lawyer and let her know what happened."

"You will not wait that long. Give her a call right now. This man is a monster and if somehow, he was able to con someone into letting him contact you, everyone involved needs to be reprimanded."

Diane agreed, and placed the call to her attorney.

"I knew it was a mistake to send that bastard to the state penitentiary," Terrez said as soon as she heard the story of the events of the morning. "Don't worry, he won't be contacting you again. I'll be placing a call to the warden of the prison right away. I can assure you, heads will roll and it's entirely possible he will be transferred to one of the penal colonies. At least that will be what I recommend when I talk to the authorities. To be truthful, I had a communication from my uncle Cassion. He called just before you did. He told me Stephen also contacted Mark. Between the two of us, someone is going to pay for letting him have a communicator, to say nothing of contacting you and Mark."

"Thank you for that."

"Another thing, I talked to one of my contacts, and they are certain they have a buyer for your father-in-law's property. It's possible you could be out from under that responsibility by the end of the week. They also think they have someone to purchase the business. For now, you and your kids can stay in your house. I told my contact you won't be ready to make the move until school is dismissed for the year. That should put your mind at ease. Also, the divorce will be finalized by the end of the month and at that time your name changes will be in effect."

With the conversation ended, Diane and her boss celebrated. "It sounds like you have one hell of a lawyer on your side."

"I do. I was shocked when I realized she was one of the aliens. Her uncle is one of the top litigators in the galaxy, or so she told me. I was shocked when I realized the Council of Intergalactic Affairs was there to represent my step-son, Mark."

"I know, I watched the trials and was impressed with Mark Almanor as well as the people who testified against your husband. It looks like you've cultivated friends in high places. I know they mentioned a place called Resurrection Ranch. Is that where you're going to be relocating once you close up your life here?"

"It is. I do have my teaching certificate, so with a little reeducation, I should be able to teach on the ranch. I'm also interested in doing the cooking for the staff and residents. I've always been a frustrated cook. Unfortunately, Stephen didn't like change. The one time I deviated from the menu he wanted followed, he beat me."

"I remember that. I know you tried to cover up the bruises, but I could still see them. I didn't say anything because I didn't want to embarrass you. I'm so glad you're putting an end to that chapter in your life."

Diane knew they wouldn't get much more work done for the day. When her boss suggested they close up the office and go home early, Diane agreed completely.

By the time Diane got home from work, the kids were just finishing up their online studies. She was glad she'd stopped at the store and bought a pre-made meal of pork chops and dressing for their dinner. Even though it was Tuesday night, she had no desire to ever make or eat enchiladas again.

~ * ~

With the evening meal completed, Buck and Terri insisted on cleaning up the kitchen before they began the job of packing up their belongings.

"I talked to my lawyer today," Diane said. "She thinks she has a buyer for your grandfather's house. Do you want to go over there and see if there's anything you want of his? It's still early."

"Can it wait until the weekend?" Buck asked. "I have a boatload of homework."

"Me too," Terri chimed in.

"That could be arranged. Maybe we can devote all day on Saturday for it. I have a feeling it will be like going on a treasure hunt."

"Does his house really belong to us?"

Diane smiled at Buck's question. "Everything both your father and grandfather had was confiscated by the state. Since I wasn't involved in any of their crimes, they turned it all over to me. At least I won't have to worry about how to finance your educations in the future. I am hoping your grandmother will be able to help me with deciding what to do with all of the furnishings."

"If we're moving out to Resurrection Ranch, why can't we get our educations there?"

"From what I know, the educational process will be in place at least through the high school level. College will be something else altogether. Your father and I always wanted you to get the best education money can buy. After meeting with my lawyer, I realized your father never set up any college funds. The money we get from liquidating everything will be set aside for that purpose."

Neither of the children said anything. All their lives they thought their father was putting money away for their future educations. Now it had been up to her to break the news to them that what they thought was going to be there for them had never been put away. It broke her heart, but there was no use in sugarcoating the truth.

They went up to the attic to begin packing their belongings. She knew there were several trunks of treasures that she'd brought into the marriage. They were things from her family that had historical value.

As soon as they stepped into the attic, she was shocked to see the trunks had been opened and ransacked. What could Stephen have been looking for?

Checking the first trunk, she saw an old photo album had been taken out and pictures were strewn across the floor. He had no right to even open the trunks, to say nothing of trying to destroy her family's history.

"Mom, come over here."

She turned at the sound of Buck's request. To her horror, she saw him holding not only a laser pistol but also an antique revolver. Beside him were two high powered rifles.

"Where did you find those things?"

Buck indicated a wooden crate. When she looked inside, she saw more guns than she'd ever expected to see in one place.

Immediately, she sent the kids back downstairs to work on their homework, while she contacted the sheriff's office on her communicator.

Vacating the attic, she went downstairs to wait for the responding deputy.

"You say you found a cache of guns, Ma'am," the deputy asked.

"Yes, we did."

"Where did you find them?"

"My children and I were working in the attic, packing up our belongings in preparation to move. My son found them in a wooden crate."

She led the way up to the attic and watched as the deputy inspected each of the firearms.

"Do these belong to you?"

"I guess you could say that, although I didn't know they even existed until my son found them."

She went on to explain about the trials of her husband and father-in-law as well as how all of their assets had been turned over to her. She had no idea there were guns in her home.

"Have you been to your father-in-law's property?"

"Not yet. We decided to work here until the weekend and spend all day on Saturday over there getting things ready for liquidation."

"I think it would be best if one of our deputies accompany you. I'm calling back to the station to have a team come out here tonight and sweep the house for other weapons that might be hidden, that you are unaware of. Perhaps you and your children would be more comfortable going somewhere else for tonight."

"We're not going anywhere," Buck said, before Diane could answer. "This is our house and since my father is no longer here, I'm responsible for my mother's and sister's welfare. "We'd like to be apprised on what you find. Legally, all of the furnishings, hidden or not, belong to us. It's not that we don't trust law enforcement, but we want to know what's being removed from our home."

When did Buck become such a mature young man? I don't know if I would have thought to stand up for my rights as a property owner.

While they waited for the team of officers to arrive, Diane placed a call to her lawyer. She decided it was best if she had legal representation during this search of her home.

To her surprise, Terrez arrived within moments of their communication.

"I didn't expect to see you so soon," Diane greeted Terrez.

"I'm sure you didn't but my husband and I live just two blocks away. I was able to walk over in no time flat."

Terrez introduced herself to the deputy and assessed the situation.

"Does the sheriff's office have a buyback program for illegal guns?" she asked.

"Yes, but…"

"There are no buts. My client had no knowledge of these weapons. She reported them to the authorities and is willing to turn them over, but not without some kind of compensation. Had the situation been different and you raided the property while apprehending my client's husband, I could see a reason for confiscating the weapons. As it is, it was my client who called you, therefore she is voluntarily handing them over to you."

Diane was actually feeling sorry for the young deputy. It would be interesting to see what would happen when the team arrived to search the property.

~ * ~

It was after midnight when the sheriff's search team finished sweeping the house. At Diane's insistence, they'd swept the bedrooms first, so her children could go to bed. Although Terri went to bed willingly, Buck remained at his mother's side offering her his support and strength of character.

During the search, three more weapons had been found. They'd been so well hidden. Diane knew she might never have found them on her own. Had it not been for Buck's accidental discovery in the attic, would she ever have found them on her own?

"Thank you for contacting us, Mrs. Cruz," the senior officer said once they finished their search.

"I'd appreciate it if you would call me Ms. Alverez. I'm in the process of divorcing my husband and changing not only my name but also the names of my children to my maiden name."

"I'm sorry, Ms. Alvarez. It's hard to know about everything that is going on in your life. My men and myself will meet you at your father-in-law's home on Saturday morning, if that's agreeable to you."

"I'd prefer to meet you there before the weekend. On Saturday my children and I are going over to the house to see if there is anything they want for a keepsake. Tonight, has been hard for them and if I can spare them any more trauma, I will."

"We'll be in touch with you sometime tomorrow to make arrangements for the search."

The look on Buck's face told her he wasn't happy with her decision to not have him present during the search of his grandfather's home.

~ * ~

Early the next morning, Diane received a communication that the authorities were ready to meet her at Michael's home. Although Buck pleaded with her to allow him to go with her, she stood her ground. School was more important and today would be the second day they would be attending classes virtually. By the end of the week, they would both be on spring break and would be able to go over to Michael's home to help her decide what to keep and what to sell.

After contacting her office to say she wouldn't be in until afternoon, she prepared breakfast for the kids. Once they were both signed on to their computers to begin their daily lessons, she left to make her way across town to meet with the authorities.

It seemed strange going into Michael's home without him being there. To her surprise, she was met by his housekeeper, Anita Gomez.

"I didn't think you would still be here," she greeted the older woman.

"I've been making arrangements to move to Flagstaff to be close to my son, but the apartment I rented isn't available for another two weeks. I thought since no one was living here, it was up to me to keep the house in the same way as I have for the past fifteen years."

"I don't know what to say. I'm the owner of the house now and my lawyer has a buyer for the property. Today the authorities are coming over to make a sweep of the house looking for weapons."

The shocked expression on Anita's face told her, the woman had no idea about what might be found within the confines of the house.

"I understand. Perhaps it is a good thing I am still here. The only weapon I know of is Mr. Cruz's laser pistol. I know where he keeps it. As for other weapons, anything is possible."

Before Diane could question Anita about what she meant, the authorities arrived before she could delve further into what might be found in the house.

The authorities were more than willing to allow Anita to lead them to the locked desk where Michael kept his laser pistol. It amazed Diane to see the large ring of keys the woman produced from the pocket of her skirt. There had to be at least twenty keys on the ring. *Why so many keys?* She silently questioned. Was it possible that each room of the house had its own key? Even so, what were the others for.

Throughout the morning, Diane followed Anita through the house. Every room had either a locked desk or safe. Although Anita seemed surprised when weapons had first been mentioned, she was able to lead the authorities to at least twenty weapons that were hidden in various locked cupboards, closets and safes.

With the weapons in tow, the authorities went up to search the unlocked attic.

"Why did you seem so surprised when I mentioned weapons?" Diane asked, once the officers were out of earshot.

"I never considered them weapons," Anita admitted. "They were just part of Mr. Cruz's private collection. He's been collecting them since before I started working here. When I first mentioned it, he told me that he was an avid collector. They were nothing more than possessions to him. The only one I ever saw him use was the laser pistol in his desk drawer, then it was only when he did target practice in the country. He also carried it when he went out, because it was for his protection."

"What are your plans for the future?" Diane asked, suddenly sorry for the woman who had kept Michael's household running smoothly for the past fifteen years.

"Mr. Cruz was always generous when he paid me. It was the same when he gave me a bonus for Christmas or my birthday. I never had many expenses, so I put the money in savings. I have enough to last me for several months if not years, until I can find employment in Flagstaff. Even if I don't find something, I am at an age where I can retire and live off my retirement funds."

"I don't know anything about the buyers, but if they are interested in having you stay on as housekeeper, is that something you would consider?"

Anita's face lit up. "As much as I would like being closer to my son, I was worried about whether or not I would have enough to do to keep myself busy. If they want me to stay on, it would be a perfect solution. If not, I will be moving to Flagstaff and the apartment my son has found for me."

The authorities came down from the attic and gave Diane a receipt for the confiscated weapons.

From just the weapons that had been seized from both properties, Diane knew she would have a good amount to put into the college funds for both of her children.

"The kids and I will be back on Saturday," she informed Anita. "They want to look through the furnishings of the house and see if there is anything they want to have as a memory of their grandfather. I thought you should know so our visit didn't come as such a surprise as it did today."

"I appreciate it. I look forward to seeing your children. I've watched them grow up ever since they were born. I love them like they were my own grandchildren."

~ * ~

Buck and Terri were waiting for her when she returned home.

"How did it go?" Buck asked.

Diane showed him the receipt she'd received from the officers and he let out a low whistle. "Wow, I thought Dad had a ton of weapons. What he had here can't hold a candle to Grandpa's stash. How did you find them all?"

"Anita was invaluable. She knew exactly where they were all kept."

"Anita? Is she still there?"

"At the moment, she has no place to go. Her son is looking for an apartment for her in Flagstaff, but it won't be ready for another two weeks. I told her I'd talk to my lawyer and see if the new owners would be receptive to keeping her on as their housekeeper. It's been the only life she's known for the past fifteen years. I do feel sorry for her."

Both of the kids nodded their agreement. She knew they thought of Anita as family. She'd been in their lives ever since they were babies.

~ * ~

Saturday was an emotional day. Anita greeted them and had freshly baked cookies as well as cold glasses of chocolate milk as a morning snack.

"I've done some more looking around and found another safe that I never knew existed. I contacted the authorities and they came right over to open it. Although there were no weapons in it, we did find a lot of papers. I think you should look over them. It seems there is more property than you thought. I found a deed for a vacation home in Mexico, as well as shares of stock in various companies. Lastly, I found this." She handed Diane a briefcase. "I haven't opened it, but I'm certain the combination will be 111148. It's his birthday. He used it for everything that needed an access code."

Buck took the case from his mother's hands and dialed in the combination. As soon as he put in the last number, the latch released. To their amazement, once the lid opened, the interior was filled with bundles of cash. Each bundle had a wrapper indicating it contained ten thousand dollars.

"I've never seen so much money in my life," Buck exclaimed. "What do you think we should do with it?"

"I think it should be divided two ways. Half will be put into our bank account and the other half should go to Anita."

"Oh, no," Anita said. "This money belonged to Mr. Cruz. Now it belongs to you. I'm not…"

"Since it belongs to us," Diane said, "it is ours to do with as we please. Consider it a bonus from Michael. You don't need to tell anyone about it. Besides, if you hadn't found it, we would have never known it existed. You deserve it for all of the years you served him so faithfully."

"I don't know what to say. Thank you. With this added to my savings, it will make my decision to retire much easier. If the new owners don't want to retain me, I will be financially secure."

Diane hugged the woman who had been such an important part of her family. She knew she'd done the right thing in giving Anita half of the money, but knowing she wouldn't see her again once they moved to Resurrection Ranch made her sad.

By the end of the morning, each of the kids had selected a memento to remind them of the grandfather they'd known and loved, not the monster he'd been described as at the trial.

"I don't know what your future holds, but once you are settled, whether here or in Flagstaff, send your contact information to my lawyer." Diane told Anita.

She reached into her purse and pulled out one of the business cards Terrez had given her. She knew it was best if her husband and father-in-law's associates had no idea where she went, once they left Arizona behind forever.

Chapter Six

Anna Manning sat in the waiting room of her lawyer's office. Ever since the trial for her former husband, she'd been contemplating the offer she'd made to Mark after the trial. She'd done her research diligently. After talking to the Montenegro brothers as well as George Little Horse, and Chester Jennings, she realized the extent of their involvement in the rebuilding of Resurrection Ranch.

"Anna, it's good to see you," Judith Nolan greeted her. "I was surprised when I saw your name on my client list for this morning. I hope nothing is wrong."

"Not wrong, only different."

"Are you talking about the Cruz trial? I saw on the news that you were a witness for the prosecution. Did you know those horrible men?"

Anna lowered her head. "I was married to Michael Cruz and Stephen was my son."

"Was?"

Anna could hear the question of horror in Judith's voice, just as she'd heard it when she told her children of the plans she was making for the future. It seemed as though everyone knew of the Cruz family, although the only one she'd confided in about her previous life was her late husband.

"My first husband was Michael Cruz and Stephen is our son. He was very young when Michael began abusing me. Those were terrible times. I threatened Michael with a divorce. He told me I could leave his home but without our son. He told me if I took Stephen with me, he would kill me to get him back. What mother, in her right mind, would put the life of her child in danger? When I did file for divorce, Michael and Stephen were nowhere to be found. I was granted the divorce and heard nothing more about either of them until I read about the trial and was called upon to testify."

The expression on Judith's face was one of total disbelief. "That means you have grandchildren you never thought you'd have."

"I most certainly do. Mark is a man now, in reality, his growth was stunted when his mother died and he was only four years old. He has big plans for his future. His friend Chris' family has purchased the ranch where the two of them grew up. They have plans to rebuild the ranch as a rehabilitation facility for the young men who also grew up there and were abused. I want to invest in this venture."

Judith sat quietly for a moment. "You have two other grandchildren, or so I've been told, as well as your two children. What about them?"

Anna smiled. "I've talked to both of my kids. They're excited about having two nephews and a niece to add to our family. They both said they would rather I spent my money on the grandchildren as they are both secure in their professions and lives. My son, David, is as excited about the plans for Resurrection Ranch as I am. Once I run the idea past Mark, he would like to be involved as well. With his background in architecture, he would be a great asset to the project. My daughter, Cindy, is also excited about the future of our family.

"That leaves Buck and Terri. They're both teenagers and this business of the crimes committed by their father is hard on them. They are both willing to change their names and move out to Resurrection Ranch. The extra bonus is that their mother, Diane, is a trained teacher. The young men who will be coming to the ranch are like Mark and Chris. They were all denied an education when they were residents of Henderson Ranch.

"From what I've learned, Resurrection Ranch will be a working cattle ranch, as well as have a superior education program and a top-of-the-line medical facility. They have the backing of not only Mark and Chris' families, but the aliens from the Denver Complex are also heavily involved. We both know how things get done when the aliens are involved."

"I should know," Judith replied. "I'm directly descended from the original aliens who came to this area. I know all the history of how we came here and the strides we have helped mankind make over the last seventy-five years. Knowing they are involved in this project means things will be happening at warp speed. So, what exactly is it you want to do?"

Anna smiled at Judith's revelation. She'd suspected Judith's family heritage in the past but never mentioned it before this.

"I want to donate to Resurrection Ranch, not just for Mark but for Buck and Terri as well. These kids need to know something good from the paternal side of their family. From what I've learned, Buck and Terri, as well as their mother, have been abused by their father. I know my ex-husband has a financial fortune. The state has asked Diane to administer his businesses as well as his accounts. Diane is planning to liquidate everything and I totally agree with her decision. She wants to put the profits aside for the children's education, but I want to also invest in Resurrection Ranch. I'd like your input on this matter. I'm planning to use some of my own money to finance Resurrection Ranch. Of course, the money from Michael's assets will be more than enough to finance Buck and Terri's education. What better use for it than to help out Mark as well."

"I applaud your intentions. You've been deprived of your son and your grandchildren for far too long. I'd be honored to handle your end of this for you. We have a good financial planner involved with our law firm. I'd like to call him in on this meeting. I can set up the legal aspects of what you're proposing while he will be able to handle the financial end of things."

~ * ~

Three hours later, Anna left Judith's office. Everything had been set into motion. From here on she would not have to worry about her monetary contribution to Resurrection Ranch and anything Diane was willing to invest from Michael's holdings. She knew she could trust Judith as well as all the members of her firm to handle distribution of the money.

After stopping for a light lunch, she made her way to Diane's home. Being spring break, she knew her grandchildren would both be at home rather than busy with school work.

It was Buck who answered the door. "Grandma Anna, I'm surprised to see you here. Won't you come in?"

As much as she wanted to embrace her grandson, she refrained. Such a show of attention would have to wait until a closer bond was established.

"Thank you. I'm hoping your mother and Terri are both here. We have a lot to discuss."

Buck led her into Diane's sunny kitchen, where her daughter-in-law and granddaughter were in the process of making cookies.

"Anna, it's good to see you," Diane greeted her. "Have you had lunch?"

"Yes, dear, I have. I didn't come here to impose on you. I merely want to let you know of the arrangements I made this morning with my lawyer."

"Arrangements?" Diane questioned. "What kind of arrangements?"

After Diane poured her a cup of coffee and put a plate of warm cookies on the table, Anna began.

"I'm certain I made it abundantly clear, at the trial, that I'm not without financial means. Since then, I've been considering your offer to have me help administer Michael's assets. I spent the morning with my lawyer and have set up a fund to financially assist Resurrection Ranch. I've also put money in trust for Buck and Terri to pay for their education. Since the three of you are in the process of changing your names and breaking all ties with Stephen, I'd like to have you move in with me in Mesa until the renovations at Resurrection Ranch have been completed. It would give you a new start without the stigma of being Stephen's children hanging over your heads. Never think, for a moment, that I would ever invade your privacy. I have a large home, with a mother-in-law suite. It was originally built on to the house for my mother-in-law. After she died, it's remained empty. Since I learned of your existence, I've been thinking of moving into it so you can have the house."

"I don't know what to say," Diane said. "This is your home. Are you willing to share it?"

"I'm more than willing. Before all this happened, I was toying with selling the house and moving into something smaller. At the time I considered moving to Dallas, where my son is and split my time between there and visiting my daughter in Peru. Now that I have family closer to home, I'm rethinking my options. I have a feeling I'm far too old to be an asset to Resurrection Ranch in any way other than financially. I do want to find something closer to the ranch in Nevada, but nothing is carved in stone as my father used to say. Anything could happen between now and when you are able to relocate. It will be a wait and see proposition."

Diane looked at her children. "What do the two of you think about Anna's idea?"

Anna was pleased to see the smiles on her grandchildren's faces.

"Like I've been saying all along," Buck said, "I want to get as far away from Phoenix as possible. Since the trials, I've had some terrible communications from the people I once thought were friends. Someone even told me I should kill myself before I became an abuser like my father and grandfather. I want to go somewhere that I can be me and not live in our father's shadow. The idea of you moving to somewhere closer to the ranch is completely out of the question. The house on the ranch is big enough for all of us to live there. Terri and I both want you to live with us."

She was surprised when Terri voiced the same opinion. She hadn't thought about the situation Stephen put his children in. Learning of their father's past and living through his abusive nature had to have been hard on both of them. Added to that was the thought the children as well as Diane wanted her to live with them on the ranch property.

"How soon do you think you can join me in Mesa?" she finally asked.

"I've already checked into our finances and started the process of liquidating both Stephen's assets and Michaels. Thank goodness I had a good lawyer. I'd been contemplating divorce for several months and together we learned Stephen put my name on everything so he wouldn't have to pay taxes on them. I've been working for several years and agreed I would pay all of the property taxes, not knowing everything was in my name anyway. He owned the house outright and was more than happy for me to pay the taxes. Little did I know his name wasn't on any of our possessions. For my children, I think we could be ready to move within the next week. I can put our furnishings in storage until we are ready to move to Nevada. I appreciate you giving us a chance to begin our new lives earlier than we ever thought we could. As far as schooling is concerned, they have both been doing their classes online. It was the suggestion of their counselors because they were being bullied at school. Their classes can continue from Mesa without them missing out on anything before the end of the year."

Anna could see the load of frustration and doubt lift from her grandchildren's shoulders. Today was a new beginning not only for them but also for her.

~ * ~

It took very little time for Anna to move her personal belongings from the main house to the mother-in-law suite. In anticipation of her newly found family accepting her offer, she'd aired out the apartment and did some painting in order to freshen up the living quarters she would be using once they moved from Phoenix to Mesa

She was also ready to put the house on the market as soon as the arrangements were made for the move to Resurrection Ranch, and the new lives they all anticipated they would enjoy.

On the day that Diane and the children were to move in, Anna made one last check of the main house. This had been her home for the past thirty-five years. Here was where she and her husband raised their children and enjoyed being empty nesters. His death, due to a tragic accident, devastated her.

For months, she'd lived in the house, reliving the past and wishing she could change the unchangeable situation she found herself in.

As she walked through the living room, she recalled the

communicator call from the prosecuting attorney asking her to testify against her ex-husband. At that very moment the past she'd buried deeply within her memory came flooding to her present.

The last thing she'd anticipated was learning she had a daughter-in-law and three grandchildren. From that moment forward, she knew she had a renewed energy and reason to live. She was ready and willing to help shape their lives.

Earlier, she'd put the picture of her late husband in the bedroom that would now become hers. At the time she spoke aloud to him, as she had every day since his passing. She'd poured her heart out to him and disclosed her plans for the future.

To her surprise she'd heard his voice within the confines of her mind.

"I wish we had known about your family before my death. I would have loved to have met your grandchildren and had the chance to spoil them. I'm pleased to think our home will be filled with young voices once again. I'm even happier to know you're thinking of selling this place and playing an important part in their lives. David and Cindy have been communicating with me in their nightly prayers and they are so excited about what your future holds, I know you're making the right decisions."

The words she heard her husband transmitting to her were the confirmation she needed. She'd always thought she was psychic, but the fact her husband had been able to communicate with her from beyond the grave only gave her further proof of her earlier suspicions.

The home security program alerted her to the fact a hovercraft was preparing to arrive at her docking station. Excitedly, she hurried to the front door to greet Diane, Buck and Terri.

"I'm so glad you were able to find my place," she said, as soon as they were walking up to the front door.

"It wasn't hard," Buck boasted. "Your directions were great and the GPS was able to follow them to a tee. Mom even let me pilot since I got my learner's permit last week."

While Anna held the door open, her family made their way into the house. She could sense their amazement at the show of wealth the house represented. She certainly hadn't looked at it that way in several years. This was her home. It was the house she and her late husband purchased together and furnished to suit their tastes over the years.

"I still don't know how you are able to move out of here to say nothing of letting virtual strangers move in," Diane said.

"I think Mark said it best. He told me Paco was a frightened toddler, Marco was an abused child and Mark is his identity for the future. This house is the life I lived with my second husband, it's where we raised our children, and enjoyed our time of being empty nesters. When he died, this house was empty and lonely. I've been ready to sell it and move on for several months now. I decided to move to Dallas to be closer to my son, but he has encouraged me to devote my life to your family as well as Mark. That along with your offer to have me share your home on the ranch, have given me a new reason to live. Let me embrace you and find the new direction that the One God has chosen for me."

She was surprised when both Buck and Terri got to their feet and came to where she was standing to embrace her. This was what she'd missed the most. When her children grew up and went out on their own, her husband filled the void in her life. Since his passing, she put on an optimistic face and didn't let anyone know how hollow she now felt.

After basking in the love her grandchildren were demonstrating for a few moments, she motioned toward the kitchen.

"I didn't know what you liked to eat, so I took a chance when I ordered food from the market this morning."

She busied herself, filling the counter on the top of the island with all of the fixings for sandwiches and several salads she'd ordered from the deli.

Buck was the first in line. She knew he would be as ravenous as David had been at that age. She remembered teenage boys seemed to have a hollow leg when it came to food.

"You should let your grandmother go first," Diane admonished.

"Don't be ridiculous. Growing boys need nourishment. It does my heart good to see him eat. Especially knowing the life Mark grew up living. I can't imagine children not being given enough food to help them grow."

By the time lunch was finished, Anna knew about the grandchildren's activities and goals. Terri was interested in dance and was an exceptional artist, even though she knew she would need other skills in life, she loved doing the activities that gave her satisfaction. Her long-term goals were to own a dance studio and teach young children. Anna knew she could be instrumental in helping her granddaughter in any way possible.

As for Buck, he wanted to be a veterinarian. It amazed her as to how much like Mark, Buck truly was. While Mark loved ranching, she knew he'd come to the decision he would never be more than the ranch manager, due to the delicate condition of his health. After talking to his Uncle Jon, she realized that veterinary medicine might be a perfect fit for him as well as for Resurrection Ranch.

~ * ~

Diane marveled at how quickly things moved. In less than a week, they'd packed up their belongings and transferred most of them to the storage unit she rented until they were able to make the move to Nevada.

The hardest thing was quitting her job earlier than she'd anticipated, but they both agreed it was for the best.

Terrez had negotiated the sale of the house, now that they were able to allow the buyer immediate occupancy.

Earlier in the day, she'd taken one last look at the house she and Stephen purchased together when they were first married. It was the only home her children had ever known and now it was becoming part of their past. She knew she had no regrets about selling the house and liquidating the holdings of both Stephen and Michael. What stretched ahead of her was a new life on Resurrection Ranch with her children and Anna.

Once she and the children finished their midday meal, Anna showed them the rest of the house. The sheer size of the structure was breathtaking. The master bedroom was massive, but the rooms for Buck and Terri were equally impressive. Down the hall, the fourth and fifth bedrooms had been conformed to private classrooms.

"You've thought of everything," Diane said. "I still feel as though we're pushing you out of your home."

"Ah, that's where you are mistaken. I've left the best for last." She led the way out to the back yard where a small cottage sat. "This is where I'll be staying until we can all move to Nevada. You don't know how much fun I've had refurbishing it to fit my needs."

Diane was completely awed when she stepped over the threshold into the mother-in-law suite, as Anna called it. The foyer was tiled and led into the living room with highly polished hardwood floors, accented with a brightly colored area rug. The colors from the rug were picked up in the rest of the furnishings. The kitchen faced to the south with plenty of light coming in through the glass door, the window over the sink and the skylights. From there she led them to the master bedroom, which looked more like a luxurious suite in an expensive hotel than a bedroom.

"Do you see why I don't mind leaving the big house? My mother-in-law had excellent taste when it came to the furnishings. All I had to do was refresh the paint and replace the curtains."

"It's elegant," Diane agreed. "How can you leave this behind to move to a ranch house in Nevada?"

"Very easily, actually. What I have in Nevada is something I would never have here: grandchildren. I miss having young people around me. David is busy with his business in Texas and even if he and his fiancé were to get married today, it would be a while before they could give me grandchildren. It's the same with Cindy. She has a rewarding life in Peru and has no desire to get married and return to this area. To be truthful, I've been very lonely since my husband passed. Thankfully, all of the stars aligned perfectly. I'm not leaving anything other than this shell of a house behind. For me the future looks brighter than I ever thought it would be."

Chapter Seven

Diane loved living in Anna's house. She was close enough to Phoenix to be able to make several trips to Terrez's office to sign all of the papers to finalize the sale of both properties in Phoenix, as well as the vacation homes, and the liquidation of all the businesses. With the money from all of the sales as well as from the stocks, the future for her children was guaranteed even with investing money in Resurrection Ranch.

The longer they stayed at Anna's house, the happier Diane and the kids were. It was amazing how each of her children had taken to their online classes. Without the bullying they experienced in person, their grades soared and they were much happier.

Anna was a godsend. She took over the role of grandparent and delighted in spoiling all of them. As Diane thought back on the lives they'd led before everything crashed down around them, she realized how little time she had with the kids. Stephen insisted she work a full-time job, even though he made out that he was a very rich man. While she worked, the children were in the care of a daycare center during the day and after school they attended a program at their church.

Things were so different now. Without her working, she'd been able to do the things that made them happy. They had several outings, and even took a trip to the Grand Canyon. Their outings were made even more special when Anna was able to join them in their excursions.

The school year was just winding down when she received a communication from Cassion. Although she'd been having messages ever since the trials, he'd never been forthcoming with information on when they could make the move. This communication was different.

"Anna's son, David, has moved to the nearest town to the ranch and has begun the destruction as well as the reconstruction. He contacted me this morning and said the house has been completely rehabbed. He assured me there are enough bedrooms for you and your children as well as for Anna. He also said he has furnished another room to be an office for Mark with an outdoor entrance. In other words, whenever you're ready to move to the ranch things are in place for you. He also said, the hands are looking forward to having you cook for them until a chef can be hired."

"How many men are we talking about?" she asked, suddenly wondering if her cooking skills would be up to the challenge.

"At present there are fifteen ranch hands, including four of the former residents. Along with them are two other former residents who have been working in the garden as well as helping David with the buildings by doing the interior decorating. Mark and Kara are getting ready to move there as are Dr. Gratan, Peter, Jerilyn, and the three younger boys. One of them is interested in learning to cook, so it looks like you might have your first student."

Diane took a deep breath. It sounded like a lot of work, but after being idle for so many weeks, she welcomed it.

"The kids have finished the school year, so once I make arrangements for our belongings to be delivered, we'll be ready to move. Anna is going to be putting her property on the market this week as well. She'll have to stay here until the house is sold, so she can sign all the necessary papers. If the sale of her property goes as smoothly as the properties I liquidated, I'm certain she will be joining us sooner, rather than later. I am anxious to meet David, since he is legally my brother-in-law."

"That's a relief. The ranch needs you, just as it needs your children and Anna. Hodia and I are making plans to relocate sometime in the coming week. Of course, Chris and Melian are on their honeymoon. From what I hear, they are enjoying seeing the colony under the ice cap of Antarctica. Once they arrive the real work will begin. They, along with Hodia, will be responsible for the educational facilities. Have you had time to update your teaching credentials?"

"I don't know how I managed it, but I was able to take an accelerated program online. I finished the course last week and the credentials were uploaded to my communicator. I can't get over how fast everything has moved since the trial. I know it was only a few weeks ago, but it seems like a lifetime since it happened. I'll look forward to seeing you and meeting all the others I've been only talking to, especially Hodia. I have a feeling the two of us will become fast friends."

Cassion laughed at her statement. "I know she is also anxious to meet you. I must tell you, the two of us have been mated since I last talked to you. It wasn't anything as elaborate as Chris and Melian's wedding. Being older, it was a more sedate affair. I must admit, I did enjoy watching the ceremonies performed by the priest from Melian's people combined with the service by the pastor at our church here at the complex, and the Native American ceremony of Chris' mother's family."

"It sounds like congratulations are in order. Once we all arrive at the ranch there will definitely have to be a celebration for the two of you."

Cassion's cheeks flushed a delicate shade of pink, as though she'd embarrassed him by her suggestion of a celebration.

With the communication ended, she went to give her children and Anna the news of them being able to move to ranch as soon as possible.

She didn't have to look far to find not only the children but Anna. They were all gathered in Anna's sunny kitchen, eating cookies and talking about what life would be like on the ranch.

"I thought I'd find you here," she said when she joined them.

Against her better judgement, she accepted a cup of tea along with a cookie still warm from the oven. "You're spoiling us all rotten," she declared.

"I'm told that's the job of a grandmother. I'm so pleased I can have this opportunity. You look like you're busting to tell us something. What is it, dear?"

"I just had a communication from Cassion, and they are ready for us on the ranch. He said David has been making the renovations to the main house, destroying some of the existing buildings and working on the construction of the dormitory as well as the apartment complex."

"When can we leave?" Terri asked, her voice laced with excitement.

"As soon as I can make arrangements for our things to be

delivered out there."

"Can I pilot our hovercraft?" Buck inquired.

"Not for this trip. It's longer than even I want to fly it. I talked to my brother, Connor, and he said he would be willing to fly us out there in our craft. He's looked into transportation back to Flagstaff and is ready to book a commercial flight back once he gets us settled."

"Maybe Uncle Connor will let me fly some of the time," Buck persisted.

"We'll see. I have to contact him and see when he'll be able to shuttle us out there. Once he is, we'll be on our way."

"What about you, Grandma?" Terri questioned. "Will you be going with us?"

"Not right away. Now that things are in motion, I want to put my property here on the market. Once it sells, I'll be getting a commercial flight to bring me out to be with you and help your mother wherever she needs me. From what I hear, one of the former residents is already there and is working not only on a garden but also a greenhouse. I'm told his name is Jerry and I'm anxious to be able to work with him. I do love gardening. I did a lot of it when I was younger, but here in Arizona, I've only been able to have a patio garden. In other words, I've had to grow my plants in pots. I'm looking forward to working with plants in soil, even if they are in a greenhouse."

Although Diane would have loved to stay and listen to the banter between Anna and the children, she knew she had lots of things she needed to accomplish before the evening meal. With Anna taking over most of the cooking for the family, she went to the main house and contacted the storage unit as to when they could deliver her belongings to Resurrection Ranch.

Once she was given a date, she called Connor.

"Hey Sis, what's up?"

"Our belongings are being delivered out to Resurrection Ranch on Friday. Are you available to fly us out there on Saturday?"

"You bet I am. I'm anxious to pilot that fancy hovercraft of yours. What about Buck, is he ready to be my co-pilot?"

"He's more than ready. I think he was disappointed when I told him he wouldn't be able to fly us out there. It's a long flight, but between you and me he would be able to make the trip."

"Come on, Sis, it's not that far. I checked it out and it's only about a half an hour flight. You make it sound like you're going to the ends of the Earth. I talked it over with Julie and she's going to be going with us and we're going to help you get settled. It shouldn't be an inconvenience, since you've got that larger craft. In other words, we're going to be taking a little mini vacation. We know there's an extra bedroom in your house, since Anna won't be coming out until after her property is sold."

"There won't be any furniture in there until Anna gets there. Where do you think you're going to sleep?"

"No problem whatsoever. We've got sleeping bags. It will be like camping out. We both want to make certain you're settled into your new place before we come home."

"It sounds like you have everything all worked out. The kids and I will pick you up early on Saturday morning. Tell Julie I'm looking forward to seeing her and spending some time together."

Diane ended the communication, her emotions in turmoil. With everything happening so quickly, she wondered how she would react to spending so much time with her sister-in-law. Julie was much younger than her and they'd never had much in common. Maybe this was an opportunity for the two of them to get better acquainted.

Chapter Eight

Saturday morning brought mixed emotion for not only Diane but also her children. The sadness of being parted from Anna, if only for a brief time, combined with the concern of making the trip with her sister-in-law and the anticipation of their arrival at Resurrection Ranch.

With the last goodbyes said, she allowed Buck to pilot her craft to Flagstaff where they would pick up Connor and Julie for the flight to Nevada. Ever since they'd been staying with Anna, Buck had become proficient piloting the craft and on his sixteenth birthday, in less than six months, he would be trading his learners permit for a proper pilot's license.

Perhaps she had been too hasty in contacting Connor to fly them to their new home. She'd thought it would be a fun excursion for her and her brother to spend time together. It was never her intention to spend the first days in her new home with Julie Alverez. The woman her brother married was too young to be a wife in her estimation, and from the first time they met, she knew they would never be close friends. The girl was too self-centered for her own good.

It wasn't a long flight from Anna's beautiful home to the small cottage Connor and Julie owned. After Buck expertly docked their craft, she got out to greet her brother.

"I'm so excited about being able to go with you out to Nevada. Connor said we'll be camping out in your spare bedroom. I have our sleeping bags packed. Don't get me wrong, I know we're going to be helping you get settled, but this is the first time we've taken a proper vacation outside of the state of Arizona."

Julie's statement shocked Diane. She'd expected her sister-in-law to act like the foolish young girl. Instead, she sounded like a mature woman looking forward to this new adventure as much as Diane was.

"It's going to be a bit of an adventure," Diane admitted. "From what I've been told the house has been refurbished, but the rest of the buildings are slated to be demolished. I've met my stepson, Mark, and I know there will be others like him who have been deprived of their childhood and educations. It will take a lot of work, but it has great backing and even greater potential."

"That's exactly what I've been telling Connor," Julie replied. "He's a trained chef. Do you think he would be able to take on that responsibility at the ranch?"

"I don't know, what about his job in Flagstaff?"

"He's been looking for something else. His contract runs out in September. If…"

"I'll have to talk it over with Mark and some of the others. Anna is one of the backers. I'll contact her and see what she thinks of the idea."

Julie broke into a wide grin. For the first time, Diane felt a warm feeling beginning between herself and her sister-in-law. Having her brother also working on Resurrection Ranch would be an ideal situation. Even with the gap in their ages, she'd felt as though she needed to protect her baby brother. Now he was an adult and having him interested in this new project meant everything to her. The rest of her family was excited to say the very least.

Connor quickly packed their belongings, including the sleeping bags. "Are we ready for take-off?" he asked.

"Yes, sir, Uncle Connor," Buck said, enthusiasm sounding in his voice. "Mom let me pilot on the way here. Do you think…?"

"Not so fast. I've been looking forward to this little trip. With my job I don't get to fly much anymore. Let me have my fun."

Diane applauded her brother's ease in talking with Buck. Although she knew he wanted to fly them to Nevada, she was more comfortable with Connor piloting them to their new home.

~ * ~

Resurrection Ranch was nothing like Diane anticipated. Everywhere she looked, construction was in progress. Shells of new buildings dotted the otherwise empty ground. The shining star of the property was the two-story house, that would become their home.

Gazing beyond the immediate area, she saw lush pasture land. From what she'd learned fifty years ago, the aliens had found a way to bring water to the dry desert land, making for good grazing for the livestock that were the lifeblood of what would become a prosperous ranch in the near future.

Once they were docked, she saw a young man coming toward them. His short-cropped hair told her perhaps he was one of the rescued boys who Mark had told her about.

"I'm Jerry Wallace," he said, extending his hand. "I was told you'd be arriving today. Ken has been working on refurbishing your home. He just finished it yesterday. Now they're working on the new kitchen and dining hall. Until then, I'm told you'll be cooking meals in your kitchen. I've been working on the garden as well as the greenhouse, so you'll have plenty of fresh vegetables. Of course, we have some of the best beef around and with the backing we have, you'll have only the best food to prepare meals."

"It all sounds wonderful. This is my brother, Connor Alverez, and his wife Julie. Behind them are my kids, Buck and Terri."

Jerry acknowledged Julie and Terri with a nod. He shook hands with Connor and Buck before he helped them with the luggage that was packed in the underbelly of the hovercraft.

"Oh, yes, I forgot to tell you, your belongings were delivered yesterday. Unfortunately, nothing was unpacked."

"That's okay, Mr. Wallace," Buck said, "Uncle Connor and I are looking forward to being able to unpack everything. Isn't that right, Uncle Connor?"

"That's right, Buck. It's time for the two of us to help your mom get settled."

Diane enjoyed watching her younger brother interact with her son. There was ten years difference in their ages, but they'd always been the best of friends.

As soon as she stepped foot in the empty house, Diane knew she was home. It wasn't the elegant house she'd shared with Anna for the past several weeks, nor was it the cold unloving home she shared for so many years with Stephen.

"It's perfect," she declared. "Doesn't it remind you of Grandma Alverez's home, Connor?"

"I was pretty young when she passed away, but yes, it does remind me of her house. I think you're going to be very happy here."

"So do I."

Like a little child on Christmas morning, she went from room to room, envisioning her furnishings gracing the empty spaces. The kitchen came as a complete surprise. It was a large room with a modern island and the most up-to-date appliances. In one corner was a breakfast nook. It contained a table meant to seat up to six people, for family dining.

Behind her, she could hear Connor and Buck opening boxes. Almost unwilling to leave the kitchen, she went to see what they were doing. She found them in what was to become Mark's office where boxes and furnishings had been piled.

"I can't believe the movers were able to squeeze everything into this room," Connor commented. "Couldn't they have put it somewhere else?"

"They were in a big rush," Jerry responded. "They wanted to get on the road back to Phoenix before dark. Fortunately, none of the furnishings for the office have arrived yet. At least everything is centralized here. Ken said he'd be over to help us when he finishes up for the day at the dormitory and Dennis will be here once he gets cleaned up. He's been out riding the range all day with some of the other guys. Everyone is looking forward to eating some good meals. Not that the prepared meals aren't nutritional, but they're not like having home-cooked ones."

After hearing about the treatment, the boys and men had endured at the hands of the Hendersons, as well as the slave ranches and skinhead organizations, she wondered how much they actually knew about home-cooked meals.

By noon, there was a knock at the kitchen door. When she answered it, Diane was surprised to see a young man who could only be called a Native American at the doorstep.

"I'm Charlie Little Horse, Ma'am. I know you're still getting settled, so I came to get you and your family for the midday meal. I know it's not what you're used to but it's good nutritional food."

Diane thanked him and called the others to join her in the open-air dining area. To her surprise, several young men and women were gathered.

"We knew you were arriving today, so we planned a feast," Charlie said. "The women have been working all day getting things ready and we've even prepared a barbecue for you."

Diane was overwhelmed. It had been a long time since anyone other than Anna had been excited for her to arrive anywhere. Seeing the excited young faces, reminded her of how cold and loveless her marriage to Stephen had become. All he'd ever wanted from her was sex, a cook, and the money she made at her job. Here none of that mattered.

After filling her plate, she joined several young women who were seated at one of the picnic tables.

"I see you tried the fry bread," a woman who identified herself as Karen Hawk said.

"Did I? I just tried to take a little of everything. What is fry bread?"

Karen giggled and pointed to what looked like a piece of pastry that had been fried. "It's a Native American tradition. We thought you would enjoy having a taste of our culture, since our tribal council is the official owner of the ranch."

"That's right, they are Mark's friend Chris' family on his mother's side. I am so pleased to have you include me in something so special."

"You don't understand, we're the ones who are pleased to have you here. When our husbands came here to work with the cattle, we came along. We've been doing the cooking for everyone and value you more than you'll ever know. I can hardly wait to work with you."

"I'll only be cooking long enough for us to find a qualified chef. Once that happens, I'll be teaching at the school."

"I'm also a teacher, so we have more in common than I originally thought. Along with the cooking, I've been doing some basic education classes with Dennis, Ken and Jerry on a one-on-one basis. It makes me so sad to see these men who haven't had the opportunity for a formal education."

Diane nodded. She'd heard about how Mark had been denied an education. She was grateful to the alien community at the Denver complex for setting him on a path to make up for what he was lacking.

Her conversation with Karen was so informative and intriguing, she didn't realize everyone had left, until she could see the lengthening shadows of late afternoon.

"Oh, dear, I'm afraid I've monopolized your entire afternoon and neglected my duties in unpacking and getting settled."

"On the contrary, I'm the one who has kept you occupied. It was Jerry's idea. The young men wanted to help you get settled. We all agreed your move here would be stressful and wanted to give you some time to relax."

"Relax, now that's a new word for my vocabulary. I haven't done much of that in the past few years. I have a feeling I'm going to enjoy my new life on Resurrection Ranch."

~ * ~

By the time Connor and Julie returned to Flagstaff, Diane had begun to form a warm relationship with her sister-in-law. She enjoyed getting to know Julie better and found her to be more mature than she had first thought. She knew she would miss them terribly, but when Connor talked to Anna via his communicator, they made plans for him to join the Resurrection Ranch family, once his contract was up in September.

"I think it's great that Uncle Connor is going to be coming here as the chef, but what will Mark think when he gets here?" Buck questioned. "He is going to be the ranch manager. Shouldn't that decision have been his to make?"

Diane was impressed by her son's concern for the feelings of his older half-brother. "Since Grandma Anna is orchestrating all of this, I'm certain she's been in contact with Mark. I know they were communicating before we left Arizona last Saturday. Even if he hasn't been advised, he knows we will need a professional chef. This is turning out to be a real family organization."

"What do you mean by that?" Terri asked.

"Well, we've heard about Mark's friends, Chris and Peter. Chris' Native American family purchased this ranch. They sent several men and their wives down to keep things running until Mark and his friends get things under control. Chris' white family has been financing many of the building projects and your Uncle David is working with his crews on the construction of them. Peter's family are financing the new kitchen and dining hall. In other words, we are all related, in one way or another, and want the same thing. Everyone wants to erase the dark past associated with this property."

Both of the kids agreed with her. They'd heard the stories of what transpired here in the past and knew they wanted to be part of the bright future the ranch promised.

"When will Grandma Anna be arriving?" Terri inquired.

"Not for a while. She has to finalize the liquidation of her property in Mesa. I think she's also planning a trip to Peru to see her daughter before she arrives here. In the meantime, I have work to do. The new appliances arrived today and I want to oversee where they are placed in the kitchen. With luck we can start using the dining hall as well as the kitchen by the end of the week. I'm sure everyone will be happy to have a proper dining room rather than using the picnic tables."

"I thought eating at those tables was a lot of fun," Buck commented. "When we were at home, Dad always insisted on having such formal meals."

Buck's mention of his father brought unbidden tears to her eyes, even though she refused to shed them. Stephen had made his bed and now he had to lie in it. Ever since she talked to Terrez about Stephen's unsolicited communication, she'd wondered what his punishment would be for doing such a thing.

Just a few days earlier, she'd heard that he'd been put in solitary confinement in anticipation of being transported to one of the secure penal colonies run by the aliens. It was where the worst of the worst were housed.

"Once we start using the new dining hall, I'm sure you'll find it's far from the formal atmosphere we had when we were living in Phoenix. For now, I need both of you to help out in getting tonight's supper ready. We'll have lots of hungry men to feed and even with Karen helping me, there are things the two of you can do. I have to go over to the new kitchen and oversee the placement of the new appliances."

Karen was already in the kitchen when Diane returned from the construction area otherwise known as the new kitchen and dining hall. She smiled to see Buck peeling potatoes, while Terri was washing and chopping vegetables for not only the cooking pot but also the salad.

"What's on the menu tonight?" she asked, when she came in.

"I'm using the leftover beef from last night's supper to make beef stew," Karen replied. "Thanks for sending in such good helpers."

"I should be the one thanking you. With all of the things I need to do over at the new kitchen, I'm certainly neglecting my duties here."

"Nonsense. We're all doing our part. I did hear from my husband and he told me that he heard Mark is arriving next week. Have you heard that too?"

"I had a communication from Mark before I left the construction area. The way things look, we should be able to start using it by the weekend, so we'll be up and running by the time Mark arrives. Things certainly do move fast around here."

~ * ~

By Monday morning, Diane awoke with mixed emotions. She and Mark had engaged in several conversations over their communicators, but would he allow her into his life? Even though he was a grown man, she saw him as a lonely little boy who was betrayed by his grandfather and who lost his mother at a very early age. She prayed he would be receptive to her attempt to fill the gap that had been opened so many years earlier.

She wanted to meet his shuttle from the Denver complex, but

she'd been busy with, not only preparing and serving breakfast, but also getting ready for the midday meal. She was pleased when Buck offered to meet Mark when he got to the house.

She'd just returned home and helped Terri take cookies out of the oven. If Mark was anything like Buck, he would be hungry after his trip.

"I'm glad you're finally here," Diane heard Buck enthusiastically greet Mark.

She knew she shouldn't be eavesdropping but she was anxious to hear the conversation between her son and his new found brother.

"We got here a couple of weeks ago. Mom's been meeting with Uncle David and they've come up with some fantastic ideas. She's got coffee made and Terri baked some cookies. We know you can't work on an empty stomach, but we're excited to show you what we've already done to the house."

As soon as they entered the kitchen, Diane could tell that Mark was having a hard time being in the house where he harbored such terrible memories. The look on his face reminded her of the way he looked before he collapsed at the trial weeks earlier.

"Mark, it's good to see you again," Diane said. "Come in and sit down. I've got a snack ready for you. Your uncle, David, should be here soon and together we can show you what we have in mind for this house. I know it's where we will be living, but it's way too large for the three of us. There's enough room for an office that is separate from the living quarters. I can hardly wait for you to see it."

Diane finished pouring the coffee and put a plate of cookies on the table, when David arrived.

"Has Diane showed you the office?" David asked.

"Not yet, we wanted to wait until you got here," Mark replied. "Diane thought I needed food before we took the tour. I think she had a good idea. I did need something to eat and these cookies look absolutely delicious. I can never remember eating anything but slop in this kitchen."

"I hope you're happy with what we've done with the remainder of this house. We wanted to erase all of those bad memories. This ranch is going to be a showpiece when we finally get everything done."

After eating, Diane could tell Mark felt much better. Terri and Buck led the way as they made their way throughout the first floor.

"Last but not least," Diane said, "here is your office."

She watched Mark closely as he stared at the door that closed off the room where he would be conducting the business of the ranch. She enjoyed the look on his face when she opened the door. Inside sat a large, modern desk as well as a comfortable chair. Windows looked out onto the vast landscape that would soon be filled with facilities as well as cattle in the distance. There was even a door leading to the outside so he could come and go without bothering the family.

"We are looking forward to the future," Terri said.

Her statement seemed to take Mark by surprise. "What do you mean?"

"I know you are planning to be the ranch manager," she began, "but in time you and Buck will be running the veterinary clinic. Mom and I have been talking about what the future holds. I love the detail involved in managing a ranch. In time, I'd like to take over the job and free you up to do what you'll be trained to do."

"I don't know what to say. I've been hoping one of the guys who will be working here might like the position, but if you're certain this is something that might interest you, I say why not?"

Diane smiled when Terri threw her arms around his neck and kissed his cheeks. "I was worried you'd think I was too young to make such a decision. I knew the minute we arrived here I wanted to be part of the operation. I discussed it with Mom and Buck. Needless to say, we all think I can handle it."

"This all has to be overwhelming for you," David said. "We've all come from different backgrounds and walks of life and yet this place seems to be magical. Even before Mom is due to arrive, I realized this place represents family. No matter what it was in the past, I see my family working with your uncles, to say nothing of the Native Americans who have kept this place running until everyone you've found can be brought back here. I've also been in contact with Peter's family. It was his parents who financed the new dining hall and kitchen. You'll get used to having family all around you."

"I hope so. I have to admit this is all new to me. I lived here with a lot of other kids, both older and younger than me. They weren't my family. They were a bunch of strangers who were thrown together for the good of Mr. and Mrs. Henderson. It's going to take a lot for the memories of the past to completely disappear."

Diane's heart ached for Mark. She didn't want to imagine what the survivors of the atrocities perpetuated here were living with. She'd met six of the young men who were now working on the ranch. They seemed to be coping well, but what was it they were keeping to themselves?

She watched as Mark left the house. She knew David would be taking Mark over to check out the trailers. Since Anna was due to arrive in a few days, she'd been researching what Mark would need in order to keep from relapsing, as he had at his grandfather's trial. She smiled to think of how Mark would soon be meeting with Anna and learning of the things she'd be doing in order to keep him healthy. From this day forward, she vowed he would never be without family in his life.

Chapter Nine

For Diane, her life fell into a predictable pattern. Along with Terri, Anna and Karen, they prepared three healthy meals a day. Even with the help she was getting, she was looking forward to when Connor and Julie would be arriving to take over the majority of the cooking duties. While they'd been on the ranch earlier, Julie told her that she'd been taking classes to become a chef like Connor. By the time his contract with his current employer was up, she would have graduated and would be looking forward to working in a restaurant. When Anna contacted Connor, she also hired Julie to work with him at Resurrection Ranch.

It didn't matter how much work there was to be done. From what Mark told her, Peter would be arriving with the three young boys as well as Jerilyn. She was anxious to meet all of them. Instead of working in the main kitchen, she was making a special meal for Mark's friends.

"I see you're busy making a dinner," Anna said, when she entered the kitchen.

"I thought it would be appropriate."

"You're one smart cookie. I'm looking forward to meeting Mark's friends, too. Of course, I'm also excited to get to meet the young boy who wants to learn how to cook and work in the gardens. I think Mark told me his name is Dan."

Diane nodded. "I remember hearing Mark speak about him. He also told me about a boy by the name of Brad. It seems Brad is the one who has a learning disability because of the treatment he received while he was growing up here with the Hendersons. I have a feeling these younger boys are all suffering from what they lived through while they were here. They haven't been gone for very long and the mental and physical scars are still healing. I'm so glad there is a counselor coming with them. They're going to need a lot more attention than the older men who have already arrived here. They all have different demons and nightmares. We saw it in Mark and I'm certain we will see it in Chris and Peter as well."

"I'm sure you're right. For now, I'm getting ready to meet Dan. I can hardly wait to start working with him."

Diane smiled. She knew Anna was anxious to meet with the young man who would be working closely with her. It was evident, she was adjusting well to the strange family that was forming on Resurrection Ranch.

~ * ~

It wasn't until the next morning that Diane had a chance to meet with the three young boys who'd arrived with Peter and Jerilyn. Upon their arrival, they'd been taken to the new dormitory building to get settled in with their mentors.

This morning she'd received a message from Siner, Brad's mentor, saying the boys would be finished with their counseling session and would be able to meet with her in the dining hall after the midday meal.

Throughout the morning, she'd been so engrossed in the preparations for the members of the community who would be coming in to eat in the dining hall. Earlier she'd prepared lunches to be taken out to the hands who were working with the cattle and the horses. It was certainly rewarding work, but she knew she needed more. She needed to connect with the boys who arrived yesterday with Peter and Jerilyn.

With the lunch crowd finally fed, she saw three of the aliens lingering at a table with the boys as well as Jerilyn and Peter.

"You boys must be Dan, Brad and Norman," she said when she approached their table.

Their mentors as well as Peter were on their feet as she joined them.

"I'm Ms. Diane I'm going to be your teacher. Can you tell me about yourselves? Maybe about how you feel about being back on this ranch."

She could see fear radiating from Brad's eyes. From what she'd been told, he suffered the most at the hands of the Hendersons. The abuse, coupled with the fact no one had been able to find the family he'd come from, had to have been traumatizing, to say the very least.

Dan was the first one to speak. "When I talked to Peter, he told me I'd be able to get an education, learn how to cook and tend a garden at the same time. I was afraid to come back here, but with the exception of the main house, nothing looks the same."

Diane smiled. "My family and I live in the main house now and there is nothing at all to fear about it. As for learning to cook, my mother-in-law is looking forward to meeting you and I know that Jerry is ready for you to join him in the gardens and the greenhouse. In a couple of months, my brother Connor and his wife Julie will be here to take over my duties in the kitchen, so I can start teaching at the school."

"I'm excited to get an education, but I would much prefer to be out riding with the men, like I did before they took us away," Norman said. "I liked the education I was given at the complex, but I had to be inside the protective shield all the time. I would have rather been outside."

"Trust me, there will be plenty of time for you to play outside. As for riding with the men, that can wait until you're older. I'm certain Mark and Peter will be able to find lots of things for you to do that will keep you busy. There are calves that need to be tended to and I've been told there's a cat who has a litter of new kittens and a dog with puppies. These babies will be enough to keep you busy."

Across the table, she saw tears forming in Brad's eyes. "Is something wrong, Brad?"

He wiped his nose and eyes on his sleeve. "I-If you live in the main house, is that where you will be punishing us? I don't ever want to go there again."

Diane got up and went over to Brad's chair, kneeling down to be on his level. "There will be no punishments here. Do you know what 'resurrection' means?"

Brad shook his head.

"Many years ago, the One God sent his son to Earth. At the time, the officials didn't want him here so they killed him and three days later the One God raised him to life. That is called resurrection. This ranch is like the son who died and was raised from the dead. There are many people who are interested in raising this ranch back to life. This is a new beginning for all of us. As for the severe punishments you received when you lived here before, they are a thing of the past. Can you tell me what you'd like to study when you're in my class?"

Brad shrugged his shoulders. "I'm not good with books and learning. I'd rather have a family. I liked it when we were in Denver and I could play with Jenny and Peggy. Do you think I could play with them again?"

The names Jenny and Peggy were alien to her. "I don't know who they are, but…"

"They're my half-sisters," Peter said, interrupting her. "They are relocating to a place close to the ranch. I'm certain they will be visiting often."

She was relieved to know who Brad was talking about. It also worried her to think about how he would react to the young girls after being so badly abused by Mr. and Mrs. Henderson. Mark told her of how Peter had been brainwashed to distrust women. Thankfully, he'd been given guidance by his mentor, Radon, as well as understanding by the others he'd encountered since being rescued only a few months earlier. From what she'd learned, he had the same thirst for learning that Mark and Chris did.

"Do you know about the One God, Brad?" she asked.

Again, he shook his head. "We were starting to learn about him when we were taken to Denver," Norman said. "Before that we never heard of him before. Is he real?"

"Yes, he is. I know it hard for you to believe, considering how you were brought up. I firmly believe, that the One God brought all of us together for a new start."

"Why do you need a new start?" Norman questioned.

Diane took a deep breath. She'd promised herself, there would be no more secrets in her life. "You met Mark yesterday. Well, he is my step-son. His father, my ex-husband, did terrible things to his mother as well as to my kids and me. It was because of him and his father that Mark was sent here all those years ago. When they were both convicted and sent to prison, my kids and I needed a fresh start. We changed our names and moved here to get away from everyone who knew about him and what he did to us. You see, we're all healing from things in our past. We can help one another to learn not only educational lessons, but lessons of love."

"What Diane is saying," Jerilyn said, "is that here we are all going to be family. Peter, Mark and Chris are fortunate to have found their families and having them close. The rest of us, me included, have no other family. We are all going to learn about love and family by living on this ranch. We will all benefit from the love as well as the education these people are willing to give to us. You each have your mentors, just as Peter, Mark and I do. They want all of us to grow up and be the best people we can be. Together, I know we'll all make our marks on the world."

Diane silently applauded Jerilyn for giving a much better description of the purpose of Resurrection Ranch than she could have ever dreamed of giving.

"Will we have to start school right away?" Brad asked.

"No," Peter said. "This is summer. I'm told that in the academic world, it's a time for kids to play rather than study. I'm certain you'll find plenty of things to occupy your time until the educational facility is completed and it's time for classes to begin."

With the meeting completed, the children were excused to go outside to play. Their mentors went along with them to make certain they stayed safe, leaving Peter, Jerilyn and Diane alone at the table.

"I don't know how to thank the two of you enough for helping me explain things to the children today."

"This is part of my job as a counselor," Jerilyn said. "As a child I was abused by my step-father. I was lucky to have someone turn him in to the authorities. I was blessed when the investigative team was from the Denver Complex. Hodia became my mentor and made my education her utmost project. When survivors from Henderson Ranch began arriving at the complex, I was able to use my education to become a counselor. I've been working with these children ever since they transferred from the Nevada complex. Norman and Dan are progressing well, but I'm still concerned about Brad. He suffered more than the other two."

"You've been counseling him," Diane said. "What do you see as his interests?"

"Surprisingly, he's very artistic. I bought along one of his pieces so you can see his talent for yourself."

She put the case she'd brought with her up onto the table and pulled out several pieces of artwork. Diane was impressed by Brad's depiction of the landscape he'd drawn using the view from his window as his model.

"These are exceptional. Has he seemed to excel in any of the other academics?"

"I monitored some of his classes. Mathematics isn't his strong point, but he's becoming an avid reader and is interested in geography and history. He's a lot like Peter, Mark and Chris, in that I think he has an exceptional mind. Unfortunately, he has a lot of paranoia because of the way he was treated growing up. It was hard for him to come here. I'm sure you picked up on his fear of punishment."

"I did. I hope I alleviated his fears on that front. There will be no physical punishments. I never resulted to anything like that with my kids, and I don't intend to start at this late date. Young men and boys need love more than they do punishment."

Jerilyn's communicator buzzed that she had an incoming message, so she excused herself to take the call in private.

"I'm so glad you were able to join the staff as a teacher," Peter said. "I totally agree that these kids need love and guidance along with an education."

Before Diane could respond, Jerilyn returned to the table, a worried expression on her face. "I'm afraid I've had some disturbing news."

"What happened?"

"The Kansas City Complex has been alerted to a situation much the same as what they found here, only it was little girls. There are three children under the age of eight, all of them the children of prostitutes who abandoned them into the care of their pimp. He's been grooming them for the life their mothers led. The authorities were wondering if we would be equipped to bring them here."

"Girls?" Peter gasped. "We aren't equipped for girls, are we?"

"That's what I told the people at Kansas City, but they don't have the ability to give them the education and counseling they need. They've been assigned mentors. Until a girl's dormitory can be built, they could be put in one of the trailers. If they were in a normal school situation, they would be attending in a co-educational sitting. I think it would be good for the boys as well. I told them we'd have a meeting with Mark and Chris as well as Melian, Kara and Hodia before I get back to them with an answer."

It was amazing how quickly the men and women who would be making the decision about these children were able to be assembled.

"Do you think having girls on the ranch is such a good idea?" Mark asked.

"They are in the same situation as the boys," Melian replied. "They've been mistreated and are as much in need of education and counseling as the boys. Do you want the boys to grow up with the same mistrust of women as you have? They're all young and by bringing in the girls, they can have a normal life experience. When I was their age, I went to a co-ed school and I think I was better equipped to lead a normal life and fall in love with a great guy. I know we originally thought this was going to be a place where the boys can grow into productive men, but these girls need us too. What would have happened if Jerilyn had been ignored by the people at the Denver Complex?"

Mark nodded his head. "You've got a point there. I know the three of us were brought up thinking all women were whores. If these girls were being groomed to be prostitutes, we have an obligation to help them like we've been helped since being rescued."

"Does that mean I can tell the people at Kansas City we'll take them?" Jerilyn questioned, excitement in her voice.

"You can tell them we will gladly make accommodations for these girls," Chris agreed. "There's no reason why the boys should have advantages the girls are denied. It might give the boys a better outlook on life, having girls they can interact with. Didn't you say they got along well with your sisters, Peter?"

"They certainly did."

"I just happened to think," Diane began, "Terri is interested in dance. She was talking about running a dance studio. It might be an interesting addition to the ranch. Do you think she'll have time for that once she takes over as ranch manager, Mark?"

"She won't be taking over for a while. Let her have her fun and if it becomes something permanent, we can always hire a second instructor. I think it will be good for her as well as any of the kids who want to participate."

After an hour of discussions, Jerilyn placed the communication to the Kansas City Complex to make arrangements for the girls to be transferred to Resurrection Ranch.

~ * ~

That evening, at supper, the announcement was made about girls coming to the ranch. To Diane's surprise, it was well accepted by all of the young boys and men.

"I think it's a great idea," Clint said. "If we want these kids to have a well-rounded education, it's best they learn about girls and how to treat them. The One God knows, we were never taught to respect the opposite sex. It would be a completion of the education not only for the younger kids, but for all of us. I, for one, wouldn't want these girls to be denied because they aren't male. If this ranch is going to be a new start for all."

"Well said," Cassion agreed, getting to his feet. "We are here to accommodate any young person who has been abused and denied an education. That's what Resurrection Ranch is all about."

Diane silently applauded both Clint and Cassion for agreeing to the new situation the ranch had been put into. Earlier she'd talked to Terri about the dance studio and she'd been excited about the possibility of pursuing her dream earlier than either of them ever expected.

"I'd like to say something," Buck said. "We all came here for a new start and I think these girls are coming here for the same reasons as the boys. None of us who haven't lived the kind of life that they, as well as the rest of you have, can imagine what they've been through. I believe, like everyone else here, they deserve the same chance as the rest of us."

To Diane's surprise, it was Brad who got to his feet next. "I liked playing with Peggy and Jenny. They weren't anything like what Mr. Henderson told us about girls. We would be able to become better adjusted. Ms. Jerilyn says we all need counseling in order to get over our past and become well-adjusted adults."

Diane could tell by the look on Jerilyn's face that Brad was parroting the words she'd used in their counseling sessions. It was evident bringing the girls to Resurrection Ranch would be a good thing for everyone.

"Brad is the last one I ever expected to speak up on this issue," Diane confided to Mark when they were alone later that evening.

"He surprised me too. I guess Jerilyn's counseling is doing him good. I pray we can help these girls in the same way as we are the boys.

Chapter Ten

It took two weeks for the arrangements to be made for the transfer of the girls from the Kansas City Complex to the ranch.

On the morning they were to arrive, their transport was met by Jerilyn, Diane, Melian, Hodia and Terri rather than by any of the men and boys. It was decided they would be able to put the girls at ease, without intimidating them further with any of the males on the ranch present.

Diane was pleased to see the three children. They were well groomed, but there was a hollow look in their eyes, indicating the abuse they'd suffered in their short lives.

"Is this where we're going to live?" Rachael Steed asked.

"Yes, it is," Diane replied. "I'm Ms. Diane. Mrs. Melian and I are going to be your teachers, along with Mrs. Caroline and Hodia. How old are you?"

"I'm eight. Lydia is seven and Betsy is six. Master says that we were going to have to start working soon. I didn't want to do that."

"You'll never have to worry about that again," Melian promised. "Here on Resurrection Ranch, you will be loved and given the education you've been denied. We also have a wonderful counselor, Ms. Jerilyn. She will be helping you to adjust to your new lives."

"I'm Terri. I'm not much older than you are and I'm planning to start a dance studio. I hope you will be my first students."

With Terri's suggestion, all three girls' eyes lit up. It was evident they were anxious to do something fun, rather than endure the abuse they were used to in their former lives.

"Where will be staying?" Sheriday, Betsy's mentor asked.

"Until the girl's dormitory can be completed, we have trailers set aside for you," Hodia replied. "They each have two bedrooms. The way the building projects are going it should be only a matter of weeks before you can move into your permanent quarters. By the time you are completely settled, it will be time for school to start. In the meantime, there are some other youngsters here who are anxious to get to know you. Their names are Dan, Brad and Norman. I know Terri has some activities for all of you to participate in before school starts."

"We're going to help you get settled," Terri said. "Once you're moved into the trailers, we'll go over to the dining hall for lunch. I happen to know that today my mom and Grandma are serving hot dogs and hamburgers, with potato salad and baked beans."

Diane watched the expressions on the faces of the newcomers. She could tell they weren't familiar with the foods that they were going to be served.

Diane and Terri accompanied Rachael and her mentor Zakaria, while Hodia and Melian accompanied Lydia and Nova, leaving Jerilyn to go with Betsy and Sheriday.

"Is all of this for us?" Rachael asked, as soon as they stepped foot in the trailer that was to become their home.

"It certainly is," Terri assured her. "At least until the dormitory is finished. Once everyone is settled, we'll show you the boy's dormitory. Of course, yours will be a lot prettier than theirs. Boys don't care what things look like. I should know, I have an older brother. Sometimes I think he's gross."

"Terri," Diane admonished, "you shouldn't say such things about your brother."

"Why not? He can be gross. All boys are at times. I talked to Ken and he agreed with me. He said he thinks the décor for the girl's dorm should be more refined than the boys. He's been looking at decorating ideas on his communicator and has found things that will be perfect."

Diane shook her head. She knew her daughter had taken an interest in the girls who would become part of the Resurrection Ranch family, but she didn't know Terri had been conferring with Ken about how the dorm should be decorated. It made her heart feel good to think her daughter was taking on such a grown-up project with gusto.

~ * ~

Terri was excited about the prospect of the three little girls coming to the ranch. In anticipation of their arrival, she had several meetings with Jerilyn to learn how she could help them to adjust. For her they were a special project.

After helping Rachael and Zakaria get settled into their trailer, she gathered the other girls and took them to where the playground equipment had been set up. As planned, Dan, Norman and Brad were waiting for them, along with Peggy and Jenny Hodges. It didn't take long for them to pair off in teams of five for a rousing game of kickball.

It was the boys who explained the rules and helped the girls to learn how to play. Once they were all comfortable, they played as though they'd been friends for their entire lives.

By the time the sun was high in the sky, they all made their way to the dining hall for the noon meal.

Terri watched as the girls tasted the picnic fare her mother and grandmother prepared for everyone. Rather than eating inside, picnic tables had been set up outside and everything was served buffet style.

"I've never tasted anything like this before," Rachael admitted after her first bite of her hamburger.

Terri beamed at the compliment. "My mom and grandma grill the best burgers in the world. You have to eat some of the other things, too. I know these foods are foreign to you, but I'm sure you'll like them."

"The hot dogs are better than the hamburgers," Brad declared. "Besides that, my favorite is the potato salad. You'll get used to eating the good food they serve here. It's a hundred times better than what we got when we lived here before. The food we got at the complex was good, but this is much better, even if I have to eat my vegetables."

"Vegetables?" Rachael questioned.

By the tone of Rachael's voice, Terri realized the girl had no idea what vegetables were. She watched the interaction between Brad and Rachael. To her surprise, Brad suddenly became the leader, pointing out the carrot sticks, celery and radishes that were put on each plate.

Tentatively, Rachael tasted the carrot. The expression on her face was one of surprise, perhaps even enjoyment.

"This tastes good," Rachael admitted. "Everything tastes good. It's a lot better than the food Master fed us."

Terri cringed at Rachael's mention of the man who had been her abuser. She remembered watching helplessly while her father abused her mother and brother. It would have been only a matter of time before he turned his anger on her. She was thankful he'd been tried, convicted and sent away for the rest of his natural life.

~ * ~

Diane and Anna sat at one of the picnic tables, enjoying their lunch. It had already been a long day. Seeing her daughter interacting with the new arrivals warmed her heart. If there had been a worry about how the younger boys would accept the girls, they were dispelled as each boy seemed to take an interest in one of the girls.

While Brad and Rachael interacted with each other, Dan sat with Betsy. Sitting across from them were Lydia and Norman. Each pair seemed to be getting along better than any of them had anticipated.

"When will Connor and Julie be arriving?" Anna asked, breaking into Diane's thoughts.

"I had a communication from them last night. Connor's contract was up as of yesterday and Julie will finish her studies by the end of the week. They will be leaving on Saturday morning and should be here before noon. Their belongings will be something else. You know how slow some of the moving companies can be. I told them they could use one of the trailers until their apartment is ready for them to move in."

"That sounds good, but why can't they stay at the main house? There's another bedroom and…"

"I suggested that to Connor, but he shot it down. He said he wanted to have their own space, be it one of the trailers or an apartment when one becomes available. To be truthful, I will be happy to give up the cooking duties so I can concentrate on educational needs for these kids. It's been a long time since I was in a classroom. Stephen thought it was a demeaning vocation. He thought it was best if I worked for the investment firm, especially when it paid a lot more money than I would have made as a teacher. Don't get me wrong, I enjoyed what I did, but I wanted to teach kids. It's what I trained for when I was in college."

Anna sighed. "I know so little about my family. Did my son go to college?"

Diane felt a lump form in her throat. All through their marriage, she thought Stephen's education mirrored her own. It wasn't until everything blew up that she realized he'd barely finished high school and taken only one semester of college courses before he took Mark's mother away from her family.

"He told me he did, but I learned that was all a lie. He'd finished one semester before he took Connie across state lines and kept her away from her family. I honestly didn't know what he did for a living. He told me he went to the office every day, but I never knew where it was or what he did there. I always made a good salary and paid most of the bills. Of course, I never knew I was the only one paying for things, until I checked our finances before the trial. I found several accounts in his name only but the only money going into the joint account was from my paycheck."

"I can understand that. He's definitely his father's son. I remember Michael telling me I didn't have a head for keeping the household books. I never knew what we had or didn't have in our checking account. I wasn't allowed to write checks. He gave me an allowance weekly that was supposed to pay for the groceries as well as anything Stephen needed. I hate to admit it, but I was young and dumb. I thought he was protecting me. Before I left, he told me I should start looking for a job to help with the household expenses. When I said I wanted to stay at home until Stephen was in school, he beat me senseless. That was when I walked away. Like I said at the trial, I feared for my life."

Diane ached for the woman who she equated with as her mother-in-law. It was true, her marriage had been dissolved, but of anyone else in the world, Anna knew what her life had been like as Stephen's wife. She wished she could have spared her children the hell she'd lived through. Thankfully, Resurrection Ranch was giving them all a chance at a new life.

Chapter Eleven

Diane was thrilled with the way the summer progressed. Ever since Connor and Julia arrived at the ranch, she'd taken the opportunity to acquaint herself with the educational facility that had been under construction ever since her arrival.

She'd seen the original plans, but was shocked to see the addition of a professional looking dance studio next to the gymnasium.

"Do you like it?"

She turned to see David Manning standing behind her. Although she hardly knew him, he was her ex-husband's half-brother. "H-how did you know?"

"Mom told me about Terri's desire to have a dance studio. When I was talking to my fiancé, Claire, about it, she didn't hesitate in designing it for me. She's also a dancer and is studying to be a dance instructor. I've been talking to Chris and Melian. It looks like you're stuck with the two of us for the duration. I've talked to a couple of the young men who are interested in becoming architects. Since I have my degree both in architecture and education, I've agreed to start teaching classes as soon as we finish the building projects."

"I don't know what to say. Every time I turn around this project becomes bigger. I can't believe how blessed these young people are. I'm certain Terri will be thrilled with these new developments."

"I know she is. Claire is meeting with her. I just left the two of them and the way it sounds they have great plans. We know that Terri has been working with the girls who arrived this summer and they show real talent. Terri told us she's trained in tap and jazz. Claire can add ballet and is hoping Terri will join that class."

"That said, would you like to see your classroom?"

"Most definitely. It's been a long time since I've been in a classroom. The classes I took before we came here made me eager to get started. I never realized how much I missed teaching. I can hardly wait to get started."

The wing of the facility designated for the classrooms necessary for teaching not only the children but also the young adults who would be given the education they'd been denied when they were forced to do slave labor for the majority of their lives was impressive.

The room assigned to Diane was painted in cheerful primary colors. In her mind's eye, she could see the children sitting at the desks that were already placed in neat rows. Above the whiteboard was a banner depicting printed letters as well as cursive. Seeing it brought back memories of the two years she spent teaching prior to her marriage to Stephen.

In less than a week, there would be six young children occupying those desks in the morning and several young men in the afternoon and evening. After seeing the progress of the three main players in this experiment called Resurrection Ranch, she prayed the other young men would be as receptive to the rudiments of education that was being offered to them. In a matter of months, Mark, Chris and Peter had surpassed anyone's wildest expectations.

She'd been shown the other section of the facility where college courses were going to be offered. Even though they wouldn't be utilized for at least another year, they were almost ready to be occupied. In her mind she could see Mark and Buck studying to become veterinarians while other young men and women studied for various careers that didn't include ranching for a living.

~ * ~

Terri was overwhelmed when Claire and David talked to her about the dance school. This had been her dream, what she wanted to do in the future and now it was all coming to fruition.

Ever since the girls arrived at the ranch, she'd been teaching them the rudiments of dance, only they thought they were playing games. She could see real talent and now that Claire was going to become involved in the teaching process, Terri had visions of dance recitals in their future.

"You look pumped about something," Buck said from behind her. "Has something good happened to you today?"

"It certainly has. Uncle David's fiancée, Claire, is joining the teaching staff. She'll be teaching dance with me, while Uncle David teaches architecture."

Buck broke into a wide grin. "Uncle David? You've acclimated to this new family. That's good. I heard about them both signing on. This place is a bit like a magnet for anyone who comes here. I'm just as convinced as they are. Everything seems to be falling into place. I have a feeling that our brother's wedding this weekend won't be the last one on the ranch."

"That's right, I almost forgot about the wedding. There's so much going on it slipped my mind. I heard some of Chris' family is coming down from Montana to participate in the wedding. It should be interesting."

"I tend to agree with you. Theirs won't be the last wedding on this ranch."

Terri nodded. With David and Claire moving to the ranch on a permanent basis, it was highly possible they would be getting married on the property. She wondered how many more changes would be coming in the future. Whatever they were, she was excited to see how everything played out.

"Terri," she heard someone call her name and turned to see Lydia along with Betsy and Rachael coming toward her. "Can you play with us today?"

"I can at least until it's time for lunch to be served. What do you want to play?"

"Can we play dance?"

Terri smiled. To these little girls, this was a game. She prayed that in the future, they would love it as much as she did. "Miss Claire is over at the educational facility. She's going to be one of the teachers and she has a surprise to show you."

The excitement in the three girls' eyes mirrored her own at the prospect of seeing the new dance studio. Together they walked over to the educational facility.

The dance studio was beyond anything Terri ever imagined. There were bars, mirrors, and a fantastic sound system, all was ready for the students to start practicing their dance steps.

"It's beautiful," Terri said, hardly aware she spoke the words aloud.

"I'm glad you like it," Claire responded. "Are these your students?"

"We like playing dance with Terri," Betsy said. "Do you like to play dance, too?"

Terri watched as Claire dropped to one knee to get on an eye-to-eye level with Betsy. "I love to play dance. If you girls are interested, dance is going to be one of the subjects we teach at school. I'm a teacher and I can hardly wait to work with Terri to teach you all different forms of dancing. Do you like this studio?"

All three girls nodded their heads.

"Good. When school starts next week, we'll be having class two afternoons a week. I can hardly wait for our classes to start."

Terri could feel the excitement in Claire's voice. It was possible, they would make a good team working with the children in the dance studio.

Chapter Twelve

The morning of Mark and Kara's wedding dawned bright. Diane and Anna worked with Connor and Julie to prepare the food as well as the wedding cake to feed the guests.

"I like working with you," Diane declared. "I'm also grateful that from now on you and Julie will be doing the cooking for everyone on the ranch."

"I bet you enjoyed it more than you're saying, Sis. You were always a great cook."

"Maybe so, but I much prefer teaching to cooking. Anyway, everything looks great."

"I'm anxious to meet George and Nancy Little Horse as well as Susan and Robert Crow. They sent a message saying they were going to be preparing some traditional Native American dishes."

Connor no more than spoke the words, when two women entered the dining hall. "You must be Connor Alverez, I'm Susan Crow and this is my sister-in-law, Nancy Little Horse. We appreciate you allowing us to use your kitchen to make fry bread for the wedding reception. Since our people have purchased this ranch, we are pleased to be able to bring our traditions to this celebration."

Diane stepped forward. "I'm Diane Alverez, Mark is my ex-husband's son and therefore my step-son. Everything you've done for these young people has been above and beyond anyone's expectations. I've been working with Chris and Melian in setting up the educational facility. It's indeed a pleasure to meet you. Chris speaks highly of you."

"Chris is my nephew and the hurt that he's endured at the hands of the monsters who ran this ranch touched our hearts more than you can ever know. Buying this ranch for him, as well as his friends, has been the least we can do to give them new lives. Chris has told us of all the plans that have been put in place ever since the young men have been arriving to further their educations. All of the families who are involved have brought about great changes. Now, Nancy and I are ready to get to work making the fry bread for the celebration. We need to get it finished before the ceremony takes place."

~ * ~

Anna could hardly believe that her daughter, Cindy, was making the trip from Peru to Resurrection Ranch for Mark's wedding. Waiting at the docking station, she thought about the message she'd received from Cindy last night. Was it possible that she was considering returning to the States and working with the medical team at the ranch? She hoped so, but refused to get her hopes up. It was enough that David was going to be living and working on the ranch.

Cindy's hovercraft arrived, and Anna watched as her daughter disembarked. To her surprise, an older man followed her off the craft. She searched her memory to bring to the forefront, the letters she'd received from her daughter over the years she'd been in Peru.

"Mom," Cindy called as she waved enthusiastically. "I'm so glad to finally be here. I hope it's all right that I brought a guest with me. This is Pastor Joel Amundson."

Anna was taken by surprise, when the man held out his hand to her.

"Cindy has told me so much about this ranch, I had to see it for myself. We worked closely together in Peru and both of our assignments will be up at the end of the month. I spoke with my superiors and told them about this ranch. They made some calls and found out these young men will be building a church on this property. I'm here to meet with Mark, Chris and Cassion to see if they would be willing to accept me as their pastor."

"Now that's a surprise. Mark hasn't said anything to me about it, but he's so busy with the running of the ranch, as well as the wedding, it's not surprising."

"If Joel is accepted here," Cindy began, "we're planning to be married and come here as a couple. We thought about getting married in Peru, but I wanted you and David to be there. Now that we have a sister-in-law and two nephews and a niece, I wanted to wait for all of my family to be here."

Anna was overjoyed. Not only were David and Claire planning to begin their life on Resurrection Ranch, now Cindy and Joel were interested in becoming closer to her.

"I don't know what to say."

"Just tell me you're happy for us. For today, I'm anxious to meet my niece and nephews. David and I have been communicating ever since he got here. His enthusiasm has rubbed off on me. I'm going to be meeting with Dr. Gratan tomorrow and hopefully he'll be able to find a place for me either at the clinic or the hospital."

It amazed Anna how everything fell into place so perfectly. A year ago, she was looking at a lonely life, with her daughter dedicated to her work in Peru and her son working in Dallas. She'd just lost her husband and was trying to decide what to do with her life. Everything changed when she was contacted to testify at Michael's trial.

Finding Mark, Diane, Buck and Terri changed everything. When David made the decision to help with the construction of the ranch, she was overjoyed. Even more emotions were triggered when David and Claire decided to stay on to become part of the dream that had been born of a nightmare. Now Cindy and Joel were ready to commit to this project.

Never in her wildest dreams had she ever thought she would have not only her children but also her grandchildren as permanent fixtures in her life.

~ * ~

Diana sat in the spot reserved for Mark's mother. Seeing him standing with Chris under the arch that had been erected to take the place of a church altar made her heart swell with pride. She hadn't given birth to Mark, but she could feel Connie's presence surrounding her. Was it possible Mark's birth mother knew what was transpiring in her son's life and approved of her standing in as Mark's step-mother?

Although the wedding ceremony was as impressive as any she'd ever attended, nothing prepared her for the traditional Native American ceremony that followed. With Mark's dark coloring, he could have easily passed for a true member of their tribe.

The regalia they wore coupled with the pageantry of the ceremony left everyone who had gathered for the wedding in awe. Once the newly married couple shared their first kiss, everyone made their way over to the dining hall for the reception.

Earlier, Diane had briefly met Anna's daughter, Cindy, and her friend, Pastor Joel. It wasn't hard to make the connection between Anna and her daughter. Cindy was definitely a younger version of her mother.

As much as she wanted to get better acquainted with her sister-in-law, she didn't want to impose on their family reunion. She did wonder how Mark would respond to even more family coming into his life. Her own children were thrilled to have found another aunt who was hoping to join them on Resurrection Ranch.

"It's all a bit overwhelming, isn't it?" Connor asked, when he came over to her table.

"It certainly is. Shouldn't you be busy in the kitchen?"

"Between Julie, Susan and Nancy, I've been completely displaced. Those gals from the reservation can be very persuasive about giving me some time to enjoy the festivities with my favorite big sis."

"Don't you mean your only big sis? Whatever, I'm glad to have you by my side. I'm kinda the odd man out at this affair. Anna and her kids are having an overdue reunion, the Montenegros are sitting at their own table, leaving the kids and me on our own."

"Well, I'm here now to support you. Since I've been banished from my own kitchen, I plan to enjoy these festivities. Let's hit the food table, before all of the fry bread is gone."

~ * ~

For Mark, the wedding was overwhelming, to say the very least. Making Kara his wife for the rest of his life was the completion he needed in his life.

Her family accepted him and for that he was blessed. Just as he was getting used to the extended family he'd found since his rescue from the slave ranch in Mexico, he was now confronted by another aunt. With everything that was going on today, he hadn't had time to get to know her or Pastor Joel. In his wildest dreams, he never thought because of his family, the pastor who would serve their needs and the One God would come into their lives.

He decided to focus on today only. From what Pastor Joel told him, they would be staying in town for at least two weeks, before any decisions about the future could be made.

Across the room, he noticed the lost boys, as Cassion liked to call the boys and young men who were returning to the ranch. Although many of them still looked undernourished, they seemed comfortable with being on the ranch again.

"Congratulations, Mark," Jon Montenegro said.

"Thank you, Uncle Jon. I do wish my mother could have been here today."

"I know what you mean, but I could feel her presence during the ceremonies. Have you embraced Diane as your step-mother?"

"That goes without saying. She's become very important to me, as have Anna, Buck and Terri. I never expected to have any family. Now it seems my family is growing by leaps and bounds."

Jon laughed. "I couldn't believe it when Anna's daughter arrived this morning and voiced an interest in becoming part of the ranch. I hope Dr. Gratan is receptive to her joining his staff. As for Pastor Joel, he seems to be genuinely called to minister to everyone here."

"I'm anxious to talk to him, just not today."

"I can understand that. With a bride as beautiful as Kara, I can't believe you're still hanging around here and not going to your apartment to begin the honeymoon. I do realize you won't be taking a wedding trip, but I hope you'll at least take a few days off to get to know each other."

~ * ~

Gratan sat at a table with his sister, Vernal, her husband, Petro, Cassion and Hodia. Although he enjoyed being with, not only his family, but also his best friends, his mind kept wandering to the woman who'd intrigued him ever since he arrived at the ranch.

Diana Alverez was a beautiful and caring woman. She deserved only the best life could offer her, yet she was saddled with the memory of an abusive husband. Even so, the events of the past few months hadn't broken her. The fact she had teenage children was an added bonus. He liked both of the kids and would be proud to accept Mark as an added addition to his family.

"What would you think if I told you I've found someone I'd like to start courting?"

Vernal raised an eyebrow at his question. "I was wondering when you would bring up that subject, brother. Diane is a beautiful woman."

"How did you know?"

His sister laughed softly. "It wasn't hard. I've gotten to know her and have seen the way you look at her. Have you made your intentions known?"

Gratan shook his head. "She's so recently divorced; I didn't want to rush things."

"You aren't getting any younger," Petro teased. "I think it's high time you settled down. Now, why are you sitting here, while Diane is sitting just a couple of tables over?"

Gratan smiled. He'd not acknowledged the feelings he felt growing within him toward Diana until now. He prayed she would be receptive to him.

Getting up from the table, he walked over to where Diane was sitting with her brother as well as her children. "May I join you?" he asked.

"I'd be honored," Diane replied. "That said, shouldn't you be engaging with your sister and brother-in-law?"

"I've had plenty of time to reconnect and they will be here for at least another few weeks. For now, I'd rather connect with you. That is, if you don't mind."

He enjoyed the way a slight blush crept into Diane's cheeks. Maybe it wasn't too soon. At least he prayed it wasn't too soon.

"You'll have to excuse me, Sis," Connor said. "Even though those women kicked me out of the kitchen, I should go and check on them."

"Mark's cousin Juan said he wanted to hang out for a while," Buck said. "He's studying to be a vet, too."

Diane nodded her approval.

"I want to go over and see Peter's sisters, Mom," Terri declared. "Is it all right if I go over to their table."

Gratan watched as Diane's kids scurried off to be with their friends. "I hope I didn't scare them off."

"Hardly. They aren't very subtle, are they?" Diane asked. "I'm glad you came over. I was beginning to feel like the odd man out here. Mark has real family and I'm…"

"I know Mark better than you do and his feelings for you are genuine. At the moment, he's a bit overwhelmed with everything that has happened since his rescue. Of course, I didn't come over here to talk about Mark. The time has come when I-I…" he was surprised to realize he had trouble saying the words that were upmost in his mind.

"Are you saying you'd like to get to know me better? If you are, I can attest to the fact the feeling is mutual. You are a special man and I have to admit, I've been hoping to get to know you better. To tell you the truth I've been busy with the preparations for the coming school year and running the kitchen. I was also afraid you would think I was being too forward if I approached someone of your position."

Gratan smiled like a grinning fool. This woman who had dominated his dreams for weeks was saying she harbored feelings for him. He was grateful to the One God for bringing them together.

Chapter Thirteen

Cindy Manning could hardly believe how good it felt to be on Resurrection Ranch. Ever since she had learned of the extended family her mother found, she had wanted to leave Peru. At the time, her assignment wasn't finished, but when Joel said he felt a calling to come here to spread the word about the One God, her superiors agreed to her leaving. Now she sat nervously in the outer office, waiting for Dr. Gratan to interview her for a position at the hospital.

"Ms. Manning," Dr. Gratan said as he entered the room, "I've been anxious to interview you. Your resume and recommendations are glowing. I can see you will be a perfect fit for the position of director of nursing. These young people who have joined me from the Denver Complex are good at what they do, but they need more direction than I can give them. I hope you are receptive to the position."

Cindy broke into a wide grin. As much as she enjoyed working with the patients, she knew being in administration would be more to her liking.

"I'm thrilled to accept your offer. Of course, I would have been happy working with the patients, but this is more than I could have anticipated."

With her interview going in a positive direction, Cindy wondered how Joel's meeting with the young men entrusted with the running of this ranch went. She prayed to the One God for him to be found acceptable to serve the residents of this ranch as their spiritual advisor.

~ * ~

Mark sat in his office waiting for Chris, Peter and Cassion to arrive for the meeting with Joel Amundson. Without having a church building, he wondered if they were putting the cart before the horse by engaging a pastor.

"I brought you a morning snack," Diane said, entering the office.

"I honestly don't have time for this," he snapped, immediately regretting his words. "I'm sorry. There's a lot going on and…"

"I know, you don't want to take the time to look out for your health. Unfortunately, Gratan would have my head if I he found out I didn't serve you a snack."

Mark raised his eyebrow at the mention of Dr. Gratan. "Gratan? Is there something going on between the two of you? I've never heard you refer to him without calling him doctor before."

He knew he didn't have to ask the question. Buck told him how Dr. Gratan asked Diane if he could court her. He remembered when he'd asked Kara to be his girl. He hadn't thought about someone old enough to be his parents courting. Of course, Cassion and Hodia recently married, or as they called it, mated.

The question seemed to fluster Diane. Was it possible she was embarrassed by the attention Dr. Gratan was paying her?

"I'm certain you've heard the gossip. Gratan and I seem to both be attracted to each other. Since we are both adults and neither of us is married, I'm enjoying our new relationship."

"Well, I for one think it's fantastic. Everyone should be as happy as Kara and I are. From what I've learned, the One God didn't expect people to live their lives alone."

Diane beamed at his comment. He knew he meant every word of it. How could he not? In the past several months, his life had been enriched by everyone who he met.

For a moment, he had a flash of a dark thought that crossed his mind. Things were going too well. He was afraid there could be something looming on the horizon he'd never anticipated before.

A knock on the outer office door dissolved the dark thoughts he'd been having. "Enter," he called.

From the smiles on the faces of his two best friends, Mark realized they must have met Pastor Joel and they approved of hiring the man to see to the spiritual needs of Resurrection Ranch.

"When are you expecting Pastor Joel to arrive?" Peter asked.

"I wanted to talk to the two of you before he arrived. You've each had a chance to talk to him, do you think he will be a good fit here at the ranch?"

"I do," Chris agreed. "He's got a good head on his shoulders and his resume is impressive. Of course, in a few months, it's possible he'll be your uncle. I know that doesn't make any difference. The man has the proper credentials."

"I feel the same way," Peter interjected. "We all have family either working on the ranch or offering financial backing. I doubt there is anyone who would object to Pastor Joel and your Aunt Cindy coming here to lend their talents to our growing community. From what I hear, Dr. Gratan offered Cindy the position of Director of Nursing."

Mark was surprised, as he hadn't heard anything about the offer Dr. Gratan was going to make to his Aunt Cindy. It wasn't unusual, since he had little to do with the working of the hospital and if he wasn't mistaken, her interview had only been completed a couple of hours earlier.

Before he could comment, there was another knock at the office door. Expecting Pastor Joel, he nodded to Chris to open the door and welcome him to the office.

Rather than his visitor being Pastor Joel, Clint Anders entered the office.

"Is something wrong?" Peter asked.

"I'm afraid there is, Boss. I was riding the fence line and found it was cut. When I took a head count of the steers in that lot, we were missing about twenty head. Someone is targeting this ranch."

"Rustlers?" Mark gasped.

As soon as the word passed his lips, he could feel the dizziness that accompanied a low blood sugar incident. The snack Diane brought him earlier sat untouched on the desk, yet he couldn't remember what to do with it. Before he could utter another word, or ask for help, the warm darkness of unconsciousness overtook him.

~ * ~

Chris watched in disbelief as his friend's stare went vacant. As soon as the realization hit him, he noticed the untouched snack sitting on the desk.

"Call Dr. Gratan," he said.

"Call Dr. Gratan about what?"

Chris turned his attention to the woman who entered the room. He immediately recognized Cindy Manning, with Pastor Joel.

"Mark's hypoglycemic," Chris explained. "I can see he didn't eat the snack on his desk, couple that with getting some bad news about the ranch and he collapsed."

"Help me get him to the couch."

Between Peter and Clint, they carried Mark across the room, while Cindy disappeared into the adjoining house. She returned with a cold cloth as well as a glass of orange juice. At her direction, Chris helped Mark get into a sitting position.

The cold cloth seemed to bring Mark back from his unconscious state. It amazed Chris how quickly Mark regained consciousness as well as becoming coherent. Although it was not as quickly as the office filled with people. Along with Diane, Anna, Dr. Gratan, Kara and Cassion arrived.

"I should have made you eat your snack in front of me," Diane lamented.

"Don't be too hard on yourself," Kara said. "This is Mark we're talking about. At times, he forgets to do what is best for him."

"It didn't help that Clint told us about the rustling that he discovered. I'm certain the stress coupled with not doing what he should brought this on."

"Rustling?" Cassion questioned. "This is the first I've heard of this."

"That's because Clint just told us about it before Mark collapsed," Peter replied. "Our fences have been cut and we're missing about twenty head of cattle. It's something I have to look into."

"Good," Cassion agreed. "Take however many men you need. Get to the bottom of this atrocity. I'm certain the Native American hands will be of help in tracking the rustlers."

Chris felt as though he was witnessing the history he'd read concerning the 'Old West' of the late nineteenth century. "I can't believe this is happening at Resurrection Ranch. Wasn't cattle rustling eradicated over two hundred years ago?"

"I'm not the one to answer that question," Cassion said, shaking his head. "You need to talk to Caroline Phillips about it. No matter what, cattle rustling is a serious crime within the ranching community. We need to get to the bottom of this."

Chris agreed, but there was just too much happening all at the same time. Although he knew he should be concerned with what was going on at the ranch, but at this point, he was worried about his best friend's health.

~ * ~

Mark could see the confliction in Chris' eyes. "I'll be fine," Mark said. "You need to go out with Peter and the others. This ranch is our future and whether you're working in the educational department or on the range, it has to be the first priority. If we don't get to the bottom of this rustling, no matter how much financial backing we have, we could go under. We owe it to the kids we're helping to stop it before it becomes toxic."

As soon as he said the words, Mark realized just how much Resurrection Ranch meant to him. They needed it to succeed. As much as he wanted to go with his friends to assess the situation, he knew recovery from his reaction to what happened would take several hours, if not days. It wasn't the first time it happened and if he wasn't vigilant, it wouldn't be the last. Once again, he cursed the Hendersons as well as Señor Gonzales for the treatment he'd received all his life, leaving him with this weakness.

"You want to go with them, don't you?" Kara asked.

"You know I do, but I'd be a fool to get on a horse when I'm not one hundred percent. This damn illness is keeping me from doing my job. The way things are, I have to be content and let my friends do all of the real work, while I'm stuck behind a desk."

He was surprised when he saw his Uncle Jon enter his line of vision. "You're being too hard on yourself. Your job is important, but not as much as your health. Once you begin your studies to become a vet, you'll understand so much more. For now, it's best you rest. If you don't want to go back to your apartment, so be it. You can relax here. I'm certain Chris and Peter will keep everyone updated through their wrist communicators."

Mark nodded. Uncle Jon was right. He did need to rest. Even though doing the paperwork necessary to keep the ranch running smoothly wasn't what he enjoyed doing, he knew it was as essential as the work done by the men who were riding the range.

~ * ~

Riding with Peter and the others brought back memories of Chris' childhood when riding with the men and boys who kept this ranch running. The difference now being that they were all well-nourished and being given the education they'd been denied for so many years.

The cut in the fence was at the far end of the ranch. He was amazed at how easily the Native American cowboys were able to pick up the trail left by the rustlers and the cattle. Unfortunately, all of the tracks disappeared when the ground turned to the rocks of an imposing canyon.

"I never knew a place like this actually existed," he gasped.

"That's because we were never allowed to ride out this way," Clint replied. "Old man Henderson knew what he was doing when he bought this place. He chose only the best land. This canyon is on the edge of a more uninhabitable area. If these rustlers have taken the cattle into that area, they probably have the means to transport them away from here. I suggest we move the remainder of the herd back to one of the pastures closer to the ranch. This area, although some of the best grazing on the place, is too remote."

"I couldn't agree with you more. Let's get them moving. We can come back later and repair the fence."

Although Chris knew exactly what to do, he was still amazed at the efficiency of his friends who did this every day of their lives. Getting away from here was the best thing that could have happened to him. With the exception of the time, he spent with Ernst and his bunch, he gave thanks that his life had changes for the better.

~ * ~

Mark's communicator signaled an incoming message. Expecting to see either Chris' or Peter's face on his screen, he was surprised to see a grotesque mask, behind which was probably one of the rustlers.

"Today's raid was just a warning. Henderson Ranch should have never been built up again."

"Who are you?" Mark asked.

"Wouldn't you like to know? Just remember what this place was in the past. It should have been burned to the ground and subdivided rather than this. What do you think you're trying to accomplish here?"

"We're trying to make amends for the lives the Hendersons tried to destroy. Why are you doing this to us?"

With that question, the screen went dark. Mark stared at the screen for several seconds. The voice behind the mask seemed to be terrifyingly familiar. He only wished he could place it. Was this one of the young men they'd been unable to find? If that was the case, why hadn't he come to them for help rather than trying to make a mockery of what they were trying to do here?

"You have a strange look on your face," Kara said. "Did you recognize the voice behind that terrible mask?"

"I think so, but I can't quite place it. I'll have to think on it for a while. I've heard that voice before, but at this moment, I have no idea who it could be."

"Is it possible that it could be someone who grew up here?"

"I think so, but I thought we'd found everyone. At least the ones who were on the books kept by the Hendersons. Cassion said they kept meticulous records of each purchase and sale of boys, to say nothing of the money they received from the state for each one of them."

"Is it possible someone could have escaped?" Jon asked.

"I don't see how, but anything is possible. From some of the stories I've heard from the younger kids, life here after I left, was even worse than when I was here, if you can believe that."

Cassion appeared to be deep in thought. After a moment of silence, it seemed as though he'd come up with an idea of how to proceed.

"I think we need to check in with IT on this one. Since you were given your communicator at the Denver complex, I think one of our techs should be able to trace where the communication came from. Luckily, one of the best IT people I know of is Peter's mentor, Radon. I'll go his makeshift office and see what he can find out."

Mark was relieved. He was aware of Radon's request for office space to be made available to him. At the time, there were no plans that could be adapted to an IT office. It had been Radon's idea to use one of the trailers that had become available once the dormitory for the girls and their mentors had been completed. At the time, Mark questioned the prudence of such an office. Now, he was glad Radon proceeded on his own to set up the makeshift office.

"I think that's a great idea," Mark said. "I know I wasn't certain we needed an IT tech, but I'm glad Radon insisted. Since we're all settling in here, there isn't much for him to do where Peter is concerned, at least until the classes start next month."

He watched as Cassion left the office while Kara, Cindy and Diane hovered over him, insisting he eat the snack sitting on his desk.

"Okay, you three, you win. I'll eat the snack. Once I do as I'm told, I have work to do. If I recall properly, I have a meeting with Pastor Joel scheduled. We need some alone time to get acquainted."

"You drive a hard bargain," Cindy agreed. "Nevertheless, I think Dr. Gratan will agree with me when I say you should drop by the clinic for a checkup. These episodes might need some medication to keep them from continuing to happen."

"Yes, Aunt Cindy," Mark replied, giving her a mock salute.

As soon as the girls saw him eating his snack, they left him alone in the office with Pastor Joel.

"She can be a bit bossy, can't she?" Mark asked.

"You could say that," Joel agreed. "At least where someone's health is concerned. She's a great nurse and I know her superiors as well as her patients will miss her now that she is no longer in Peru. She told me that Dr. Gratan offered her the position of Director of Nursing at the hospital. In my opinion, she's a perfect match for the hospital here. Of course, that's not the reason I'm here, is it?"

"No, it's not. I've been talking to Chris and Peter. They are in agreement that Cindy is not the only one who is a good match for Resurrection Ranch. We've come to the conclusion you are exactly what we need here. We, like many of the other kids and men who have grown up here, know little about the One God. Chris and I were lucky to have been told about Him, but I doubt the others have much, if any faith. Peter is receptive, but he's moved around so much since his rescue, I doubt he's had time to come to any conclusion about the church. That said, we would like to have you join us here, if you are content to work without a church for a while. We have intended to have one built, but there are other structures we need to complete first."

Joel smiled broadly. "The church is not a building. There's an old song that goes something like this, 'where two or three are gathered in my name, there will I be'. It comes from the Bible, Matthew 18:20 to be exact. The verse is *'For where two or three are gathered together in my name, there am I in the midst of them'*. In other words, I don't need a building to spread the word about the One God and the stories found in the Bible."

"I was hoping that would be your answer. We need you here and if you're willing to work under such primitive conditions, I would like to offer you the position. As of now, I can offer you one of the trailers to use as your church."

"Since Cindy and I will both be working on Resurrection Ranch, I have an important question to ask her. I hope you and Kara will be willing to attend our wedding."

"I guess that will make you my uncle. That could be interesting. Do I call you Uncle Joel or Pastor Joel?"

"How about just calling me Joel? I remember when I was a kid, the pastor of our church was elected as Bishop. At the time I was told I could no longer call him Pastor George. My parents took me to his installation ceremony. We met him out in the hall and asked him what I should call him, his answer was 'just call me George'. I'm not a bishop, but the same thing holds for us. We are all working here for the same goal in life."

After shaking hands, Joel and Mark left the office. Mark knew there would be no more work done today and he wanted to take Joel to the trailer that would double as his church for the time being.

Chapter Fourteen

Although Radon originally thought tracing the communication Mark received would be relatively easy, he was mistaken. Even with the help of his counterparts at the Denver and Nevada complexes, they'd found it to be a daunting project. Finally, they turned to the IT department at the complex on the dark side of the moon.

When Radon received the information, he was dumbfounded. After extensive research, it was determined that someone named Simon Reason sent the message from an internet café in Las Vegas.

Radon was certain the name was a made-up one. He decided a trip to Las Vegas to visit the internet café was the next move he should make. Rather than go alone, he asked Cassion if he would accompany him for the trip. With Cassion's law background, he would know the proper way to glean the information they needed without crossing over any legal boundaries they shouldn't breach.

"What are you hoping to find?" Cassion asked.

"I honestly don't know. I'm certain there is no one by the name of Simon Reason. I mentioned the name to Peter and he didn't recognize it."

"Have you thought of contacting the police officer who found Mark when he was just a toddler? If I recall it properly, his name is Jason Culver."

"I did. I looked him up and he's working as a detective for Clark County. I sent him a message and he responded. He said he'd meet us at the café for lunch. I'm hoping he can help us."

They told no one of where they were going, so as not to get up the hopes of the young men who were working so diligently to bring new life into Resurrection Ranch.

It didn't take long for them to locate the internet café. It was Cassion who first recognized Jason. The officer was in what looked like an intense conversation with the owner of the café.

"Jason," Cassion said, getting the man's attention. "I'm glad you were able to meet with us today."

Jason turned. "I'm happy to help. How is Mark?"

"He's coping. More and more of his family have come to the ranch to live and work, so he's no longer alone in the world. He's also struggling with his medical condition, but that's not what we've come here for."

"I understand. I've been working with the Las Vegas police force on this one. They have a unit that investigates cybercrimes. This does fall under that category, at least in part. This is Keith Pelton. He's the owner of this café."

Radon assessed the man who had just been introduced. He was approximately thirty to thirty-five years of age and stood well over six foot tall. It was possible he was descended from one of the original alien families who had come to Earth many years earlier.

"I'm hoping the information I have here will be of help to you in identifying Simon Reason. When someone signs into one of our computers, it's usually so they can contact people without giving away their true identity. In this day and age, personal communicators can be traced much more easily than when someone uses our facility. That being said, we make it a practice to take a photo of everyone who signs in. Our customers don't know this, but as soon as they sign in, the computer takes their picture and saves it along with their name. I'm hoping this helps you."

Radon took the hard copy of the picture from Keith. He looked to be close to the same age as some of the young men who were now working and living on Resurrection Ranch.

"We do thank you for your cooperation," Cassion said, as he studied the picture Radon held in his hand. "Hopefully, one of the young men on the ranch might recognize him."

At Keith's insistence, they ordered lunch and spent the next hour discussing the complexities of the rustling incident as well as the message sent to Mark the same day from this café.

~ * ~

Mark was concentrating on the books for the ranch when his communicator indicated an incoming message. He was surprised when Cassion was his caller.

"Why are you calling me?" he asked. "You know my office is always open to you."

"Radon and I are in Las Vegas checking out a lead on the rustling incident. We've found out who sent the message to you, but we're certain the name he used is a made up one. Does the name Simon Reason mean anything to you?"

Mark thought for a minute. "It doesn't ring any bells. I don't remember anyone by the name of Simon being at the ranch when we were. Is that who sent the message?"

"That's the name he gave at the internet café. They have a picture of him. I know you saw an image when he made the call, but he was disguised. The owner of the café gave me a better photograph. I'm bringing it back in the hopes someone there will recognize him.

"Radon and I also met with Jason Culver and he sends his regards. He asked if he could come out to the ranch to visit and I told him he was welcome any time he wants to come. That got me thinking. With the rustling going on, we could use a security officer. Think about it, but I think we should offer him the position."

"I hadn't thought about it, but it does sound like a good idea. I don't know if he'd be receptive, but it's worth a shot. I'll talk it over with Chris and Peter. Between the three of us we are certain to come to the right decision."

They ended the communication, leaving Mark with more questions than answers. Unable to concentrate, he closed the books he was working on and made his way to the Educational Facility. With any luck, he'd be able to confer with Chris about what Cassion suggested.

As he walked across the common area of the ranch, he noticed Terri working with the younger children teaching them some of the games they should have learned in early childhood. At the moment, they were playing duck, duck, goose. His inner child wished he was young enough to join in the fun, but he had other more pressing things on his mind.

The Educational Facility was a beehive of activity as the teachers were busy getting classrooms set up for the opening of school within the next month. Mark found Chris with Melian in the administrative office, conferring with Hodia.

"Have you got a minute to talk?" Mark asked.

"Sure, Buddy. The girls can handle things here and I could use a break."

Together they walked outside so they could talk privately. "So, what's up?"

"Did you know Cassion and Radon went to Las Vegas today?"

"Las Vegas? Why there? I doubt either of them are gamblers."

Mark laughed at Chris' observation. "Radon was working with the IT departments at the Denver and Nevada complexes to find out more about the communication I received on the day of the rustling. I guess they weren't successful so they contacted their counterparts on the dark side of the moon. Whoever found it, they traced the transmission to an internet café in Las Vegas. That was why they went there. The owner was able to give them an unmasked picture of someone calling himself Simon Reason. They're bringing a copy of the picture back with them to see if any of us recognizes this guy. You know I thought I recognized his voice, but couldn't place it. It's possible this is someone who might have been here when we were and we haven't found him yet."

"It makes sense. I don't recall anyone named Simon Reason, though. Of course, it could be a false name. A way for him to remain unknown. It won't hurt for several of us to look at the picture and see if we recognize him."

"There's another thing. They met Jason Culver while they were there."

Chris looked perplexed at the mention of Jason's name. "I'm not sure I know who he is."

"He's the police officer who found me when my mother died."

"That's right, I guess I'd forgotten his name."

"Anyway, Cassion thinks we need a security officer. He asked me how I felt about offering the job to Jason. I wouldn't be opposed to it, but I wanted to run the idea past you. With having a security officer, it would take one more thing off our plates."

Chris pondered Mark's suggestion for a moment. "It makes sense. Do you think he might be interested in the position? I mean, I doubt we can offer him anything close to what he's making now."

"I have a feeling he might. You have to realize working here, he would get the best medical treatment available to say nothing of a place to live rent-free and any meals he wanted to enjoy at the dining hall. That means a lot in this day and age. It's also possible he's close to retirement age and would be eligible to receive his pension. This could be a good way for him to ease into retirement and still have enough money to live on for the rest of his life."

"When you put it that way, it does sound like a good idea. Do you know how to reach him?"

"I don't, but I'm certain Cassion does. Let's wait for him to get back. That will give us time to talk to Peter about this and get his take on the whole thing. After all, he is the foreman. He's the one who is most interested in what goes on out on the range. Sure, you're the ranch manager, but you're not out there riding with the men on a daily basis. The way I see it, he's in more danger than either of us. We do need to get his opinion on it."

Mark felt a load lift from his shoulders, to say nothing of his mind. He found he had the bad habit of second guessing himself when it came to decisions about the ranch. Talking things over with Chris as well as Peter allowed him to have his friends to act as a sounding board when making important decisions.

In the distance, Mark saw the hovercraft returning to the docking station at the far end of the common area. Anxious to see the picture they were bringing with them, Mark hurried to be at the station when they disembarked from their craft.

~ * ~

Radon studied the picture Keith gave them when they were at the internet café. "I hope someone at the ranch can identify this man. I'm having my doubts about it being Mark, Chris or Peter, though."

"What do you mean?"

"It's hard to judge age on Earthlings, but I'm willing to bet this man is older than those three. It's possible he'd closer to the age of Ken, Dennis and Jerry. They're about five years older than Mark, Chris and Peter. It's a possibility they'll be able to identify him."

"You might be on to something. We can make it a point to talk to them after tonight's evening meal. The sooner we catch this guy, the better."

Radon agreed with Cassion. "I agree. I heard you talking to Mark about the possibility of hiring Jason Culver. Do you think he was receptive to the idea?"

"I think so. He said he wanted to talk it over with Peter and Chris. I don't blame him, it's a big decision. Even though Mark has ties to the man, he's wise to talk to the others about it. This is something that will be of interest to everyone on the ranch."

Radon knew if it was Peter they were talking about, he would be just as protective as Cassion was of Mark.

As soon as they landed, Mark was there to meet them.

"I thought you'd be up at the office," Cassion said, once they disembarked.

"I couldn't concentrate. I was anxious to see the picture of the man behind the mask."

"I doubt you'll recognize him. Radon and I estimate his age about five years older than you. We're hoping one of the older men can identify him."

Cassion watched Mark closely. He was certain Mark thought he would be able to identify Simon Reason. Unfortunately, he was just as certain that Mark wouldn't recognize the man in the photo they brought back from Las Vegas.

~ * ~

Cassion's comment about the fact Mark might not recognize the picture they brought back from Las Vegas, bothered him. Since the voice sounded vaguely familiar to him, he prayed he would recognize the face.

He wasn't surprised to see Chris and Peter waiting for them at the office. It was evident they were as anxious to see the picture as he was.

"I told Mark we doubt if you will recognize this man," Cassion began. "We judge the man's age to be about five years older than you are."

"I still want to see it," Mark said. "We all want to see it."

Mark watched, anticipation growing within his mind and body, as Cassion pulled the picture from its protective envelope.

"I don't know him," Peter said, shaking his head.

Mark and Chris both agreed.

"Maybe we should show this picture to the others," Chris said. "Of course, I doubt if anyone else will know him either. Most of us haven't been rescued long enough to look that healthy and well fed."

Mark took a second look at the picture. He had to agree with Chris. Although Chris had been rescued longer than any of them, he still didn't look as healthy as a twenty-one-year-old man should look. He hadn't been starved like Peter, the others, or even himself, although he was suffering from malnutrition. It was entirely possible that this man was, somehow, related to one of the past residents of Henderson Ranch.

"Can we make copies of this picture so we can show it to some of the others?" Mark asked. "I'm certain none of the younger kids would know who it is, but we need to talk to at least six other men who have come here. They're all working now, but we can talk to them tonight when we finish eating."

"That sounds like a good idea," Radon agreed. "There has to be some connection between this man and someone who was raised here."

Mark took the photo to the printer to make copies. The more he stared at the face looking back at him, the more he felt as though he'd seen it before, but where? Like Chris pointed out, the man looked too healthy to have ever lived through the atrocities that had been perpetuated at the hands of the Hendersons.

~ * ~

As the men and boys came into the dining hall, Mark handed out the pictures, explaining about this being the man who threatened them after the rustling.

"If I didn't know better," Clint began, "I'd say this was Jake Rawlins. He was a year or two older than me. He once told me he'd been brought to the ranch because his mother was a dirty whore."

Peter immediately joined the conversation. "Did he ever say who the man was who brought him here?"

"It was a funny name, Dale, Dallas, something like that."

"Could it have been Delos?"

"That's it, he called him the bad man."

"What happened to him?" Chris asked.

"Don't you remember? He was one of the kids who died in the punishment box. Maybe he was one of the lucky ones. He didn't have to live the life we all lived both here and at the ranches in Mexico."

Mark immediately recalled the day Jake was taken to the punishment box but never returned. Jake had to have been about fourteen or fifteen at the time. Older than Mark and his friends. Like so many others, he was there one day and gone the next. Suddenly, he was no longer hungry for food but for information. Hidden in the books kept by the Hendersons had to be something about Jake and what happened to him.

"Just where do you think you're going?" Chris asked, as Mark turned to leave the dining hall.

"I need to check out the ledger kept by Henderson. It's got to say something about Jake."

"Even if it does," Peter said, joining the conversation, "it will still say the same thing after you eat your meal. I'm interested in it too, because Delos was the one who brought me here. I'm now wondering how many other kids he sold to Henderson before my old man killed

113

him."

Although Mark was anxious to dig into the files in his office, he knew it was best not to argue with his friends. After all, they did have his best interests in mind. He'd be foolish to skip a meal in order to go through the ledgers and computer files kept by the Hendersons.

~ * ~

Mark always considered his office to have ample space, but now it seemed terribly crowded. Along with the nine adult survivors of the ranch, Cassion, Radon, Melian and Kara assembled, helping Mark to look over the record books.

"I think I have something," Peter announced. "This ledger says that Henderson bought Jake from Delos for ten thousand dollars four years before he brought me here. I wonder how many other kids that old bastard kidnapped and sold. From everything I heard at the trial for my father, he wasn't the brightest bulb in the pack."

"You forget," Radon said. "Delos Reynolds was one of the kids raised here in the early days. He might not have been intelligent, but he knew enough to see a good deal when he saw one. For him it was easy money. I have a feeling kidnapping you was his idea and your father ran with it. Of course, he had no idea this was something Delos had been doing for years. It's probably the reason he was killed. That way he couldn't tell anyone what your father did to you. Nonetheless, it's all nasty business for certain."

"I've got another journal. It says that Jake had to be punished and was sent to the box for fifteen hours," Chris said. "That would be one hour for every year of his age. It also says he didn't survive and was buried behind the box with the others."

"Let me see the date on that journal," Mark requested. "I can look up the information from the state to see if he continued to receive funds for him."

Mark pulled up the file containing the ledger for payments from the state. While Mr. Henderson kept a handwritten account of the daily running of the ranch, Mrs. Henderson must have kept the books. Each page had the name of a different resident. Looking under R for Rawlins, the page with Jake's name was one of the choices that came up. It indicated the ten thousand dollars paid to Delos Reynolds, followed by monthly stipends from the state until three years after Mr. Henderson recorded Jake's death in his journal.

"I don't even want to look any further. It could take us years to go through all of the journals and seeing how many kids died in that box. To say nothing of how many years they defrauded the state out of money to pay for the keep of kids that were dead and buried."

"What I don't understand is if Jake was dead that long, how would any of his family know to interfere with what we're doing here?" Peter asked.

"I can answer that," Cassion replied. "When we started unearthing the bodies behind the box, we were able to identify many of them through their DNA chips. Even if the bodies were nothing but bones, the chips were still intact. We were able to do the research necessary to find the majority of the surviving families. Each family was contacted and told what happened to their loved one. Of course, like many of you know, we weren't able to find all the families. In the morning, I'll contact the Denver Complex and see what information we can get on the family of Jake Rawlins."

"Cassion is right," Kara agreed. "We can't do much until morning. So far, we haven't had any other losses. It's best if we all get a good night's sleep. Tomorrow could be a very busy day, depending on what Cassion learns when he talks to the research team in Denver."

Mark nodded. He knew his wife was right, but he also knew sleep wouldn't come easily tonight. He had far too much on his mind to consider sleeping peacefully. From the looks on the faces of his friends, he knew they would be in the same position, especially Peter. Knowing that Delos Reynolds was behind the kidnapping and selling of young boys to Henderson must have been disturbing to him. All his life, he'd cursed Delos for what he'd done to him and now he knew he'd done it to others.

Everyone slowly left the office, leaving Mark and Kara to lock up.

After shutting down the computer and turning off the last light they left the office without putting back the journals that now littered the desk as well as the small table and every chair in the room. He knew he could clean it up in the morning.

By the time they reached their apartment, they found Aunt Cindy and Pastor Joel waiting for them.

"Dr. Gratan contacted me," Cindy greeted them. "He had word from Cassion. What you learned tonight has been upsetting. I've got a sedative for you."

"I don't need to be sedated to go to sleep. When did I become Dr. Gratan's special project?"

"Not so special. There are other nurses going to Chris' apartment as well as to the dorm to make certain all of you get a good night's sleep tonight."

"I agree with Dr. Gratan," Kara said. "No one who hasn't lived through the nightmare of growing up here can understand how you're feeling. Being there tonight when you found those records about Jake, I could see all the old hurts coming to the forefront of all of your minds. A sedative will help you get the rest you need to address this problem in the morning. Tracking down Jake's family and putting an end to their harassment of Resurrection Ranch, won't happen overnight."

Mark reluctantly agreed and after getting ready for bed allowed Cindy to give him the sedative. While he expected a sleepless night or at best one filled with nightmares, the sedative did its job. He enjoyed a peaceful night's sleep.

Chapter Fifteen

Peter mentally thanked Dr. Gratan as well as Radon for ordering the sedative. He was afraid he wouldn't be able to sleep but with the sedative, he woke more rested than he had in a long time. After his morning shower and shave, he dressed for a day on the range, even knowing he wouldn't be riding with the men today. He wanted to find out what he could about Jake Rawlins.

He barely remembered Jake, as he was older and not within his circle of friends. The Hendersons were very strict about not mixing with kids who were either older or younger than themselves.

Since last night, he'd done some thinking about Jake. He remembered him as an angry teenager. Now knowing of Delos Reynolds and his part in supplying children to Henderson, he wanted to know how many more kids were exploited by the man. Today, he wanted to look at the ledgers on the computer to see if Delos was mentioned in the acquisition of other kids.

By the time he got to the dining hall, Chris and Mark were already sitting at a table. They looked as rested as he felt.

"I assume you both had a visit from someone at the hospital last night."

Mark laughed. "Aunt Cindy told me Dr. Gratan was sending people to every one of us. I was upset about it, but when she said you were being given sedatives too, I gave up arguing. Today is going to be trying. If the two of you are like me, you want to go through the journals as well as the ledgers."

"Do you think they'll be able to locate the Rawlins family?" Chris asked.

"I don't put anything past Cassion," Mark replied. "Remember what he said about last night contacting the families, at least the ones they could find, for the kids they found buried behind the box. It shouldn't take long for him to get in contact with them. Hopefully we'll know more by the end of the day if not the end of the week."

Peter remained quiet. As much as he wanted to put an end to the harassment of the ranch, he worried about meeting Jake's family. They would be able to tell him more of Delos Reynolds. He wondered how anyone could be so wicked as to sell children to Henderson, especially considering they'd learned he'd been raised here in the early days of the ranch.

Together they went up to the buffet table. Peter was surprised to find he was ravenous. Everything looked better this morning than it had any previous days of his life.

"Your plate looks like it would feed all three of us," Chis teased.

"I don't know what they put in that sedative, but I'm literally starving this morning."

"I know what you mean," Mark agreed. "After Clint identified the picture last night, I lost my appetite. I ate enough to keep my wife happy, but not as much as I would usually consume. We've all had a lot to digest since last night. Something tells me, you and the others will be helping out at the office today. Thank goodness several of the Native American cowboys decided to stay on. They can handle things, especially since having most of the cattle and horses moved in from the outlying ranges. We're going to have our hands full going through all the journals and ledgers."

Peter was relieved to know Mark was comfortable with him working at the office today. There was so much information he hoped to glean from the journals. The ledgers, although they were interesting, were nothing more than numbers. He had no desire to know how much money the Hendersons made off of the boys they raised to be sold as slaves.

~ * ~

.

Cassion met them at the office and assigned each of the nine young men a journal to go through. Since the ledgers were all on the computer, Cassion took over the job of going through and printing off copies of everything he found.

Chris knew the ledgers were important, but he was more interested in what the journals had to say. It was amazing to see all of the handwritten material detailing the everyday running of the ranch for the decades the Hendersons were in charge.

"FIRE!"

Everyone dropped what they were doing and hurried outside to see flames coming from one of the barns. From all over, people came with hoses and buckets, knowing the fire department in the next town wouldn't arrive for several minutes.

By the time the fire department arrived, the immediate danger was behind them, but the professionals were kept busy putting out small flare ups and watching for fires to start in adjoining buildings.

"Was anyone hurt?" Chris asked.

"Jerry and Dan were in the barn getting the gardening supplies to start working in the garden," Dennis Salinger replied. "They both suffered from burns and smoke inhalation. They're over at the hospital and Dr. Gratan is taking care of them. There was a man there that none of us knew. It's possible he's the one who started the fire in the first place."

Chris studied Dennis closely. His face was covered with soot from the fire, but through it, Chris could see a burn on his left cheek.

"Let's go over to the hospital. I want to check on Jerry and Dan as well as the man who possibly set the fire. While we're there, I think you should get checked out. It looks like you might have suffered a burn to your cheek."

Dennis put his hand up to his cheek. It was apparent during the excitement of fighting the fire, he hadn't noticed the pain before Chris mentioned it.

The hospital was a beehive of activity. It was apparent there were more people injured than just Jerry, Dan and the man who could have started the fire. Two of the Native American cowboys were also there with minor burns as well as Dan's mentor Felton.

As much as he wanted to check on everyone, he left Dennis at Urgent Care and went to where the mystery man was being treated by Dr.

Gratan as well as Cindy Manning. The man had burns over forty percent of his body, including his face, making facial recognition next to impossible.

"Is he going to make it?" Chris asked after getting masked and gowned up.

"He will, but it will be a long recovery. We read the DNA chip and sent the results to Denver for any match they could make."

"Will we be able to question him?"

"Not for a while. We've put him in a medically induced coma to keep him out of pain."

Chris shook his head. As much as he wanted to get to the bottom of why this man set fire to one of their buildings, he knew any questions he might want to ask, would have to wait.

Instead of waiting for what could be hours if not days, he went to the area of the hospital where the others were being treated. He was thankful when he saw none of them were as severely injured as the unconscious man in ICU.

~ * ~

Hodia stared at her computer. The information she just received from Denver confirmed what she and Cassion suspected. The DNA for the man who supposedly started the fire matched that of Jake Rawlins and his family.

She engaged her communicator and called Cassion.

"Have you received any word from Denver?" he asked when he answered her call.

"I have. Thankfully, they had all the information on Jake Rawlins family on file. It looks like he's either Jake's brother or a close relative. I have all the information to contact the family. Do you want me to contact them?"

"I think that would be a good idea. If this is their son, or another relative, they will want to be here by his side. Do you have information on where they live?"

"It's in the file they sent me from Denver. They're in a small town in Iowa, Maquoketa to be exact."

"Good. Tell the family we will be sending a hovercraft to pick them up. It's imperative that they get here as soon as possible."

Hodia agreed with her husband and placed the call to the number listed for the Rawlins family communicator. After only a moment, the face of a middle-aged woman filled the screen.

"Is this Patsy Rawlins?" Hodia asked.

"It is, but you have me at a disadvantage. I don't recognize either your face or your voice."

"I'm sorry, my name is Hodia and I'm calling you from Resurrection Ranch in Nevada."

"Is this about Zander?"

"If that's your son's name, it is. There's been a terrible accident and he's in the Intensive Care Unit of our hospital. Our administrators feel it's imperative you get here as soon as possible. We have already dispatched a hovercraft to pick you up. They should arrive at your location within the next two hours. Can you be ready to leave by then?"

"We most certainly can. We lost one son to that horrible place. We don't want to lose another to it."

"I'm not a mother myself, but I can understand your concern. When you get here, you will, hopefully, learn what happened here in the past and what we are hoping to achieve in the future."

With the communication ended, Hodia sat quietly for a moment. She prayed to the One God that Jake and Zander's parents would be able to shed some light on why their son was trying to sabotage what everyone was trying to accomplish here.

~ * ~

Cassion waited at the docking station for the return of the hovercraft he'd sent to Iowa to bring the Rawlins to Resurrection Ranch. Although he knew he had lots of questions that needed to be answered, he also understood the Rawlins were concerned about their son. Their feelings had to be addressed before there could be any further questions posed.

The hovercraft docked and Cassion watched as the older couple, along with a young woman disembarked.

"I'm Cassion," he said, extending his hand in greeting.

"I'm Vern Rawling. This is my wife, Patsy, and our daughter, Josie. The woman who contacted us seems to think our son, Zander, is here."

"That would have been my wife, Hodia. We were able to trace our patient to you through his DNA chip. I'm afraid he's in serious condition. There was a fire and…"

"…and my son set the fire. It doesn't surprise me. He's been fired up ever since we were told that Jake was dead because of this damnable ranch."

"Vern, please, we can talk about this later," Patsy pleaded. "We need to see our son. We need to let him know we're here for him."

"I agree, Mrs. Rawlins," Cassion said. "I'm here to escort you to the hospital. You'll find everything on this ranch is within walking distance. My wife is making an apartment available for you. I'll let her know you will need one with two bedrooms."

Cassion could tell Vern Rawlins was seething, but like his wife said, they could talk about it later. At the docking station he saw Roger Blount waiting to take the Rawlins' luggage to the apartment complex.

By the time they arrived at the hospital, the earlier excitement of treating the patients who were suffering from either burns or smoke inhalation had quieted down to almost a normal level of urgency.

After taking the Rawlins to the Intensive Care Unit, he went to check on the other people who had been injured in the morning fire.

How could this have only happened this morning? It feels like a week slipped past in the last few hours.

"You look deep in thought," Dr. Gratan said, silencing Cassion's silent ramblings.

"I guess I was. How is the Rawlins boy doing?"

"It's going to be a long rehabilitation, both mentally and

physically. The boy had to be mentally confused in order to come onto this ranch to set fire to the barn after rustling our cattle and taunting Mark about it."

"I have a feeling there's a lot more to it than meets the eye. Mr. Rawlins is almost belligerent about being on this ranch. Especially since one of his sons was trafficked here by Delos Reynolds."

"Delos Reynolds, that's a familiar name."

"It should be. He's the man who instrumented the kidnapping of Peter and later brought him here. We've got a lot of ledgers to go through, but I think he was supplying Henderson with boys in order to defraud the state and keep this ranch running until he could sell them to the ranches in Mexico or the militant groups up north. After he kidnapped Peter, he was killed. In other words, Henderson's pipeline for new kids dried up abruptly."

"From what I heard, Mark was sent here by the state after Peter arrived and there were other kids who were sent here after that."

"It's possible we'll find more of the kids who were brought up here in the early days were also doing the same thing as Reynolds. We've got a lot of ledgers and journals to go through before we know exactly where Henderson was getting the kids who were brought here."

~ * ~

"He looks so bad," Josie pleaded. "Are you sure he's not dead."

The nurse who was tall and light complected with violet eyes, turned her attention to them. "I'm Kara Almanor, your brother's nurse. He's doing as well as can be expected. He has some very extensive burns. Dr. Gratan has put him into an induced coma because of the pain. We've sent for one of the best burn specialists in the galaxy. Luckily, he's at our St. Louis Complex and will be here tomorrow morning. He'll be able to start the reconstruction of the burned skin while your brother is still unconscious. I'm told it's a painful process, so it's best if he remains in a coma until it's complete. Are the three of you planning to stay for the duration? I'm certain Hodia has arranged for accommodations for you at the apartment complex."

"We are," Vern replied. "I can work from anywhere and be damned if I'll allow my only remaining son to die on the godforsaken ranch."

"I understand about your loss, Mr. Rawlins, but I can tell you this is no longer a godforsaken ranch. My husband and the other young men who grew up here and were rescued are trying to make this into something to be proud of. We have an excellent education program as well as a working cattle ranch. Most of the young men who have agreed to come back here are interested in learning more than just ranching. Once my husband completes his formal education, he plans to study to become a veterinarian. Whatever any of the young men and boys want to study to become, the administrative staff will make it happen. I'm sorry for what happened to your son, but we are trying to make a difference here."

"You'll have to excuse my father. He's been bitter ever since we were told that Jake was killed on this ranch, at least on this property when it was owned and operated by the Hendersons."

Josie watched the expression on Kara's face. It was evident she was well aware of all of the atrocities that had been committed on this ranch. Since she was definitely one of the aliens, it was possible she'd cared for one or more of the survivors.

"How is it you know so much about this ranch?" she finally asked.

"My husband was raised here and sold as a slave to one of the ranches in Mexico. I saw him after he was first rescued and brought to the Denver Complex. You might think I'm uncaring, but it is better your brother died rather than have to experience the same things as the other young men and boys who were rescued. Most of they were suffering from malnutrition, dehydration, and mistreatment at the hands on of ranch owners who bought them from Mr. Henderson. My husband, Mark, has health problems that make it impossible for him to do the things he loves, including riding the range with the other men. He's the ranch manager and thanks to his family, he plans to start his studies in veterinary medicine soon."

"You mentioned others." Patsy said. "How many are there?"

"At this time the ranch is centering its attention on those survivors who have no family, at least none that have been found. The exceptions are my husband, as well as his friends, Chris and Peter. They were some of the first ones to be rescued and brought to our complexes for treatment. Chris was the first and he told us about Mark. Once they started raiding the slave ranches, they found Peter, as well as three of the others. The three youngest ones were on the ranch when it was raided and the three oldest had been sold to one of the skinhead groups. We are working on DNA to find their families, but so far we haven't found a match."

"If your husband and his friends have found their families, what are they doing here?" Vern asked, his tone one of anger.

"I can tell you about Mark, but I think you should talk to Peter and Chris about their reasons for being here. Mark was more dead than alive when he was brought to Denver. Through the trial for the Hendersons, he was reunited with the police officer who found him when he was just a toddler. His mother had died, and they were using an assumed name. They had no way of finding his family. Once he was rescued, Cassion insisted he be given a DNA chip. That was when we started to find his family. First, we found his mother's side of the family. His Uncle Phil is helping out with the financial backing of the ranch, while his Uncle Jon is setting up a veterinarian office as well as an educational program for young men to study to become vets.

"When everything came to light, it was evident Mark's mother was not only murdered, but also kidnapped and taken across state lines while she was still a teenager. Cassion insisted that Mark's father and grandfather be arrested and charged with her kidnapping and murder. At that trial, Mark met his father's second wife and her children as well as his paternal grandmother. Once we were ready to move operations here, they all relocated here as well. Diane, Mark's step-mother, has a background in education and she is working with Chris and Melian to get the school set up. His grandmother, Anna, is financially backing the ranch and has moved here to be closer to Mark and his siblings."

"You did mention your husband has half-siblings," Vern said. "Why would they want to move here?"

"They were from Arizona. The trials for their father and grandfather were quite sensational. They were being treated badly by their friends. Since the trial, they have changed their names and decided to move here with their mother. They will be afforded the best education available. Buck has decided he wants to study veterinary medicine with Mark and his sister, Terri, has an interest in becoming the ranch manager. They will both be given the proper education in order to follow their desires."

"Are the stories of all of the survivors this dramatic?" Patsy asked.

"Pretty much so. It's not my place to tell you about them, but I'm certain they will be more than happy to meet with you. The younger children, of course, won't be able to speak to you without their mentors with them. There are three young boys who were rescued from here and three young girls who were rescued from another trafficker who was grooming them for the sex trade."

Josie wiped her eyes. For years she'd thought only of her older brother who had been ripped from his family and later died on this ranch. She'd given no thought to other children, who were now men, who suffered the same fate in life. Hearing there were little girls who had been kidnapped and groomed for lives as prostitutes, made her absolutely sick to her stomach.

"Did any of them know my brother?" Josie questioned, her voice hardly more than a whisper.

"You'd have to talk to Clint Anders about that. When Cassion and his friend Radon went to the internet café in Las Vegas where your brother sent the message to Mark, they were given a surveillance photo. Although, Mark, Chris and Peter couldn't identify him, it was Clint who said he thought he was looking at an age-progressed picture of Jake. Of course, before anything could be done, the barn was on fire. Dr. Cassion read your brother's DNA chip and that was how we were able to contact your family."

Josie digested everything Kara told them, while her mother

thanked the young nurse for filling in a few of the gaps. She could tell her father was still seething, anger boiling just below the surface. She prayed he wouldn't act on his anger, and come to realize that, although Jake died on this property, something good would be built here.

Chapter Sixteen

Mark closed up the office for the day and headed toward the dining hall. It had been a trying day. The fire brought to light the name of the man who had been behind the rustling and the threatening message. He knew that Hodia had contacted the family and they'd arrived. He probably should have met with them, but his duties in the office overshadowed everything else.

He'd met with Uncle David about rebuilding the barn and authorized the purchase of the necessary supplies in order to begin construction.

Once the fire was extinguished, he'd watched the bulldozing of the smoldering remains and clearing the ground for the new structure to be built.

All in all, it had been exhausting. Thankfully, Grandma Anna brought him a midafternoon snack, which he took the time to eat. He certainly didn't want a repeat of the attack on his body of just days earlier.

He was pleased to see Kara waiting for him. "How are things going at the office?" she asked, when she came to his side.

"Busy. We're just waiting for the supplies to arrive for rebuilding the barn. How about things at the hospital? Are any of the patients badly injured?"

"I thought maybe you'd be over to check for yourself. Our people have only minor injuries and they're recovering. Unfortunately, the man responsible for the fire is in a serious condition. We did identify him through his DNA. His name is Alexander Rawlins. Cassion had his parents brought here and they call him Zander. His brother was Jake Rawlins, just like Clint thought. I know there's a story there, but the father is very angry. I can't blame him."

From the corner of his eye, Mark saw Cassion enter the dining hall with three strangers. "Are those people the family?"

Kara nodded. "I talked to them in ICU when they came to see their son. The young girl is their daughter, Josie. The parents are Vern and Patsy."

"I think I should speak to them. Can you introduce me?"

Together they crossed the room and Kara made the necessary introductions.

"Did you know my son?" Vern asked.

"I vaguely remember him. He was older than me. We were encouraged to stay with kids our own age. Clint knew him, so did Parker and Roger. I'm certain they would be more than willing to tell you about him. From what we've been able to find in the ledgers and journals, Henderson was punishing Jake. Because of his age, it went too far. I remember several of the kids just disappearing. There were never any explanations. One day someone was there and the next day they weren't. We may not have been properly educated, but we did know enough not to ask questions."

"What do you mean because of his age?" Vern questioned.

"We read it in the journals. Kids who were punished were put in a box for one hour for every year of their age. Jake was fifteen, so he was in that box in the hot sun for fifteen hours."

"Were you ever in the box?" Patsy asked.

Mark could feel bile rising in this throat and tears pooling behind his eyes. "It was right after I first came here. I told them I was hungry and wanted more to eat. I was paddled and put in the box for four hours. I learned early on not to complain about anything again."

Tears ran down Patsy and Josie's cheeks at his description of the punishment box.

"I'm sorry to be so graphic. I should have had more consideration."

"Don't ever be sorry for telling the truth," Vern said consolingly. "It takes a lot of courage for you to talk about what had to have been hell on earth for you and the others who were brought here. I was ready to take up where my son left off and burn this place to the ground. After talking to Nurse Kara and Cassion, I can see you are trying to erase the bad and build up the good of this place."

"I won't detain you any longer. Help yourself to the buffet. I'm certain, in time, Cassion will set up a time for us to meet. I know Peter, Chris and I would like to hear about how Jake ended up here."

Vern shook hands with Mark, as did Josie and Patsy. He felt sorry for them. They would never have the chance to reconnect with their son as he did with his extended family. Would they have been as accepting of the uneducated young man who might have been brought back into their life? They might have at first, but without an education and possible medical problems he might have encountered in later life, he would never be the child they lost so many years earlier. In his heart, he knew he should be happy he survived, but his life on Henderson ranch as well as a slave in Mexico, left a bitter taste in his mouth.

~ * ~

"I saw you talking to Jake's parents," Peter said, as they took their seats at his table. "Did they know anything about Delos Reynolds?"

"I don't know. We didn't talk about that. I'm afraid I said more than I should have regarding how Jake died. I did tell them that Clint, Parker and Roger all remembered Jake and they should talk to them. To be truthful, I didn't even think to ask about Delos."

"I guess that's something we should address with them," Chris said. "I've been reading the journals and until Peter came, he was bringing in one to two kids a year. After Peter arrived, he isn't mentioned anymore. Of course, we know what happened, but it sounds like Henderson was confused as to why Delos wasn't bringing in more kids."

"The deeper we delve into this, the worse things get. It's hard telling what other secrets we'll uncover in the next days and weeks."

"Let's talk about something else," Melian suggested. "The school is ready to open. All of the teachers are in place, and we've started testing the older survivors. It seems that Ken, Dennis and Jerry have a leg up of the others. Someone in the skinhead organization they were part of had been working with them. They're ready for an accelerated secondary school education. As for Clint, Parker and Roger, they got help while they were in the facility in Mexico. They have a few more tests to pass before they're up to the same level as the others. We're making good progress with you younger kids. They're almost up to grade level. Even Brad is doing well. We have Jerilyn to thank for that."

Across the table Jerilyn blushed at the compliment. "Peter helped a lot with him as well. The way I see it we're all in this together. Everyone helps out in different area. One isn't more important than the others. Is it possible we can set up a meeting between the Rawlins, and all of us, including all of the adult survivors? I don't think including the children would be in their best interests."

"I agree," Melian said. "Other than the fire, the little kids don't know anything about Jake or Delos for that matter. I've been meeting with them but it's hard to get them to talk about how they happened to be sent to the ranch in the first place."

Peter totally agreed with Jerilyn. She knew the little kids better than any of them. It was even possible that they might never remember how it was they came to be at the ranch. His own nightmares kept the details of how and why he arrived at Henderson ranch alive.

"Do you have room for two more at your table?" Cassion asked.

"You know we do," Peter replied. "We were talking about setting up a meeting between us and the Rawlins."

"I think that's a good idea. Radon and Dr. Gratan are joining them for the evening meal and filling are them in on what they know about Zander's condition."

"I'm told you talked to them when they first arrived. Did you ask them about Delos?" Peter inquired.

"I did, but they have no idea who he is or was. They're victims as much as you and Jake were. I can't imagine the pain they went through not knowing what happened to their son. I've talked to your mother, Peter, and she said she wants to meet with them. She knows what they're going through. I'm certain she can be more comforting to them than any of the rest of us. I do have to tell you: Vern is very bitter. If he could, I think he'd join his son in trying to destroy this place. We all have our work cut out for us to make him see what we're trying to accomplish here."

~ * ~

"What do you think about this place now that we've been here for most of the afternoon and evening?" Patsy asked.

"I'll withhold judgment until we have a chance to meet with more of these young men. What's to keep them from doing to others what was done to them? I mean, how many times have we heard about how someone who is brought up in an abusive household becomes an abuser? Can anyone guarantee the older boys might not do things to the younger ones?"

"Oh, Daddy," Josie said, "from the people we've met today, I can see that they're looking to change this place for the better. They were all terribly abused. I was talking to Radon after dinner and he told me that Peter was brought here by the same man who kidnapped Jake. He told me how Peter was sold as a slave and branded like the ranchers brand their cattle. I thank the One God that Chris was in that group protesting at the Denver complex. It was because of him that the ranch was raided and the young men who were at the various ranches in Mexico were rescued."

"I guess the aliens have been doing a good thing here," Vern conceded. "I do like Dr. Gratan and the nurse who was taking care of Zander when we got here. It's evident they're both Aliens. I'll be anxious to meet this burn specialist they're bringing in. It does bother me that Nurse Kara is married to one of the survivors of this ranch. Of course, growing up under those conditions, he probably doesn't know any better than to intermingle with those people."

"Those people," Josie echoed. "You sound like the radicals who didn't want people to marry because of race or the sexual preference. From what I learned recently, that's one of the things that brought this country to its knees in the early twenty-first century."

"I never heard that," Patsy commented.

"Of course, you haven't. Up until that woman was found in suspended animation out in the wasteland of California, no one was teaching it. I learned about it from one of my college professors. He was able to get me a transcript of the history she brought to the forefront. It's fascinating. There is so much that none of us ever learned. Even though I've already graduated from college and am ready to begin my teaching career, I'm thinking of continuing my education to take some history courses. I'm hoping someday I can find Caroline Phillips so I can study under her. Can you imagine going to sleep for a hundred years and waking up to a whole new world, where no one knows anything about the past?"

"Don't get your hopes up. Who knows where she is being kept? It's possible she's under wraps at one of the alien complexes. She's much too important to allow her a normal life."

"I agree with your mother. I thought sending you to college was a waste of time and money and I don't see any reason why you should even consider going back for further classes."

Josie knew her mother made sense, but she had hopes of finding out everything she could about the woman who had opened the eyes of the entire country to what the past had once been. As for her father's opinion, she dismissed it as she had for her entire life. He'd never approved of her getting a college education and probably never would. She refused to allow him to continue to ruin her life with his warped ideas.

Chapter Seventeen

Peter was up early. He needed to look into the journals Chris had been going over for the past few days. By the time he got to the office, Mark and Chris were hard at work reading the journals and the ledgers left behind by the Hendersons.

"I figured you'd show up here today," Mark greeted him. "What can we get you?"

"I'd like to look at the file for Jake Rawlins. Henderson did keep files on all of us, didn't he?"

"He did," Mark confirmed. "We haven't had a chance to look it over yet."

Mark held out the thick file folder. Once Peter took it, he was surprised by the weight of the contents. Was it possible all of them had such complete files?

While Mark worked on the computer and Chris sat on one of the wing backed chairs, Peter took a seat on the couch, laying out the contents of the folder on the low table in front of him.

The first picture he picked up was of Jake at probably the age of three or four when he was first brought to the ranch. A note on the back of the picture said that Delos Reynolds brought him from Maquoketa, Iowa and was paid ten thousand dollars for him. From the trial, Peter remembered that Delos had been paid thirty thousand dollars for him. He must have raised his price, or perhaps it was his father's idea that they ask for more money. It surprised him to think that the man was willing to split the profits when before he was able to get the entire amount for himself.

Each year there were pictures progressing Jake's age, but he didn't look as healthy as he had in the first picture. Each year the weight was recorded and it didn't go up in the way it should. By the time he got to one of the later pictures, Peter recognized the boy who was older and had taught him how to rope a steer when he was first starting to ride with the men. There had been so many older boys, he had trouble remembering all of their names. Perhaps it was selective memory or just the fact he was so engrossed in his own reason for being on the ranch that he didn't care. He certainly didn't mingle with the older boys as much as he did those of his own age. It was the way Henderson wanted things.

"I just had a communication from Cassion," Mark said, breaking into Peter's internal ramblings. "He wants us to meet him in the dining hall in ten minutes. Are you up to meeting with Jake's family?"

"I guess I have to be. After looking at these pictures, I did recognize Jake. He's the one who taught me how to rope a steer. I can't remember if I even knew his name."

"We understand. Remember we were brought up here, too. I didn't know the names of those who were older or younger than us. It was that way purposely to keep us in the dark about who was here if one of us escaped. We're all lucky Chris was rescued and remembered that many of us were sent to ranches in Mexico. Once all the pieces fell into place, Cassion and his people were able to rescue all of us."

"You're right, of course. I just feel bad that I didn't remember him when I first saw his brother's picture from the internet café."

"Don't beat yourself up over this," Chris advised. "It's only natural that most of us blocked out the things that went on here."

Peter agreed. Although he dreaded the meeting with Jake's family, he knew it was necessary for them as well as for him.

~ * ~

Josie and her parents arrived at the dining hall after the last of the morning diners left to go about their daily activities.

They'd stopped at the hospital first, but Zander was still in an induced coma. They did meet with the specialist who arrived late last night from St. Louis. He assured them that he expected Zander to make a complete recovery, but it would take a long time, considering he would need several skin grafts. He explained a new technique he'd developed using artificial skin that was working wonders with patients like this.

It didn't take long for several young men to arrive. Josie wondered if any of them were the ones who knew her brother better than anyone else in the world.

"These young men were all at the ranch at the same time as Jake," Cassion began. "Chris Laughlin, Mark Almanor and Peter Hodges were younger than Jake."

Each of the young men shook hands with all of them, before taking seats at one of the long tables.

The next young men who were introduced were Ken Rapier, Dennis Salinger and Jerry Wallace. Josie realized they were much older than her brother would have been. After shaking hands with them, she turned her attention to the last three men.

"This is Clint Anders. He was the first one to recognize Zander as looking a lot like Jake. His identification was confirmed by his friends Parker Flint and Roger Blount."

"Why couldn't the others recognize him?" her father questioned.

"I'd like to answer that," Peter said. "It was Henderson's policy for us to only know the kids who were our own age. It wasn't until I looked into Jake's file this morning. I recognized one of the last pictures of him, because he was one of the older kids who taught me how to rope a steer. I never knew what happened to him until all of this came to the forefront. He would have been working and bunking in a different area from my friends and me. Of course, when someone disappeared from the ranch, we all knew better than to question where they went or why."

Josie tried unsuccessfully to hold back her tears.

"I know it's hard to recognize all of us at this time, but I'm Clint. Jake was one of my best friends. Unlike our friends who are younger and older than us, Parker, Roger and I knew what happened to him. He'd broken one of Henderson's made-up rules and was sent to the punishment box. At his age, it was possible he would never come out of it alive. We were aware that he'd died and was buried behind the box with the rest of the kids who were punished and didn't survive. We also knew to say anything would jeopardize our own lives. Like all of the others who died during this punishment, we understood it was best if we forgot about them. We did as we were told or we would be buried alongside them to be forgotten by everyone who knew us."

Tears were running down Clint's face. Even knowing he was the same age as Jake would have been, she marveled at how much older he appeared.

"What can you tell us about the day Jake disappeared?" Peter inquired. "Cassion told us you didn't know Delos Reynolds. He was the man who procured kids for this ranch and was paid handsomely for doing so. I should know, because he was the man who sold me to Henderson."

Josie watched as she saw her mother nod. "We were at a church picnic. Jake was playing with some of the other children and I was busy with the women of the church. Zander felt he was too old to play with the little ones so he was playing baseball and Josie was just a baby. When the younger kids returned, our Jake wasn't with them. They didn't know what happened to him. Of course, they were all three and four years old. After that we didn't hear anything about our son until we were contacted by the people in Denver that they'd found him buried on this ranch."

"That was when Zander and I realized this place should be destroyed for what they did to my son and his brother. We thought everyone associated with this hellhole should be punished."

"Now that you've been here and met us," Mark began, "how do you feel about Resurrection Ranch?"

"I don't know how I feel. My youngest son is dead. I never got to see him grow up or go through puberty. I didn't get to take him to his first day at school, see him go to his first prom, or get his pilot's license. That was all stolen from me. I didn't know if my son was dead or alive for almost twenty years. I realize now that my older son was taking out our anger on those who not only survived but were trying to make a difference here. If my older son survives his injuries, I have no idea what will happen to him. Will he become another victim of this place?"

~ * ~

Peter could understand Mr. Rawlins' concerns. He knew his

mother had suffered not knowing what happened to him for all those years. Unconsciously, he rubbed his upper left arm where he'd been branded after being sold to the ranch in Mexico.

"I can relate to the suffering of your family. In due time, I hope you'll be receptive to meeting my family. We were fortunate enough to be reconnected with them after too many years apart. I haven't talked to anyone else about this, but considering your son's injuries, I hope something can be worked out. If he still has our cattle and is willing to tell us where they are, they can be returned to us. As for the arson..." he choked up, unable to say anything further.

The arson as well as the rustling had hurt the ranch, but not completely crippled them. Insurance would cover the replacement of the barn. If they could get the cattle back, they would be made whole.

"I agree with Peter," Mark said, coming to his rescue. "Your family has suffered because of the actions of the Hendersons. From what Dr. Gratan tells me, your son's recovery is going to take a long time. Both he and my wife would like to have him remain here for rehab. I've also talked to Cassion and we agree if we're made whole, something could be worked out to keep from pressing charges. As of now, we haven't involved the county authorities in this. All through this, we've hoped to handle things internally. We're determined to be as self-sufficient as possible."

"Are you saying you won't press charges against our son?" Patsy questioned.

"If the cattle are returned to us and we're made whole, no, we won't, but we will insist he stay here for his rehab," Cassion replied.

The Rawlins seemed to be relieved, but Peter could see additional questions forming in their minds.

"How did you know the name of the man who kidnapped my brother?" Josie asked.

Peter knew, as much as it hurt him to admit it, he had to tell Jake's family of his journey to Henderson Ranch.

"When I was three or four years old, my father kidnapped me. It was his friend, Delos Reynolds who brought me to this ranch and sold me. Once my father had the money in hand, he murdered Reynolds. These are all facts I've learned since I was rescued from the ranch in Mexico where Henderson sold me as a slave. As all the information came to light, it was found out that my biological father was not only a kidnapper but also a serial killer. He was tried at the Denver Complex and sentenced to life without parole on the penal colony on the dark side of the moon. They told me my mother was a dirty whore. I believed it completely until I was reconnected with my biological mother. It was part of the lies that were told to most of the kids who were raised here."

"My story is different," Chris began. "My father was killed in a hovercraft accident before I was born. My mother died of her injuries after I was delivered by C-Section. It's the same with Mark. His mother was dead and no one knew who his father was. That being the case, there was no need to poison our minds against women. Those people did a lot of damage. From the journals, we've learned that it was customary to tell the kidnapped kids that they'd been taken away from their parents because their mothers were dirty whores. It made it possible for them to accept the life they were forced to live on this ranch."

"You mentioned journals," Vern said. "Do you mean to tell me that monster kept a written record of what he did here?"

"He did," Mark replied. "Cassion's people found them when they first raided the place, but no one delved into them until Clint mentioned Zander's resemblance to Jake. Since then, we've been going through them as well as the ledgers. Mr. Henderson kept meticulous records. It will take weeks or even months for us to go through them all. The ledgers told how much he paid for each of the boys that were brought here by Delos Reynolds and a couple of other men who grew up here when it was a legitimate boys ranch. He also recorded what he received for them when they were sold to either skinhead groups or the ranches in Mexico. They paid ten to thirty thousand dollars for each boy and sold them for thirty to fifty thousand dollars. We worked as unpaid labor until we reached the age of eighteen. Considering what they were making from selling the cattle as well as the kids who turned eighteen, they were getting quite a bargain."

Josie and her mother wept openly while Vern discretely wiped at his eyes with the back of his hand.

As much as Peter ached for them, he secretly envied Jake's premature death. *How much easier would it have been to have died rather than be sold and branded as a slave?* He immediately regretted his silent question. If he'd died while in Henderson's care, he would have never known the truth about his mother, nor would he have met his sisters. His destiny had not been to die on this ranch but to bring it back to life.

Chapter Eighteen

With the start of the school year, each of the older students were given the hours they were expected to be in their classes, either before starting their work for the day or after they finished. Peter's classes were scheduled for early morning. After finishing his accelerated history class, he made his way to the corral to saddle up his horse for their day of riding the range with the men.

"Peter," he heard Mark call from across the compound. "I'm glad I caught you before you rode out for the morning. Can you come over to the office?"

"Sure thing. What's up?"

"It's best we discuss this in the office. No use in everyone on the ranch knowing what I need to talk to you about."

Peer hurried over to the office. Suddenly, he was apprehensive about what Mark wanted to talk to him about. He was certain it wasn't his work ethic or the way he was supervising the hands. Whatever it was, he knew he would soon know what was going on.

He was surprised to find Chris, Cassion, and Radon waiting for him. "I must have really screwed up," he said. He hoped he sounded like he was joking.

"Not at all," Radon assured him. "We've uncovered some information I thought you would be interested in. Delos wasn't the only one who was supplying boys to Henderson. There were three former residents of the ranch who were bringing kids here. It could be only the tip of the iceberg, but it's something we should advise the authorities about. I have the names of the other two."

Peter took a seat, certain if he remained on his feet, his knees would give out on him. He'd been relieved to think that the only monster supplying boys to Henderson Ranch was dead. Now he knew there were others who were as terrible as Delos Reynolds kidnapping kids and bringing them to the hellhole they called home for most of their lives.

"So far, we've identified Foster Warren and Noah Hammer as two boys who were among the first to be raised here. They were the same age as Reynolds and they aged out at the same time. From the most current journals, Warren brought Dan here shortly after Noah brought Brad. These men have to be found and tried for their crimes."

"Dan and Brad? Are you certain?"

"Positive. They are part of the pipeline bringing kids to Henderson. It's all in his journal. At the end he wasn't paying as much for each of the boys. It looks like they were only paying between five and ten thousand a kid. I think Henderson was getting desperate to get new kids, but didn't have the money to pay top dollar like he did when Reynolds brought you and Jake here."

"Is there anything in those journals that indicates where Brad and Dan could have been when they were abducted?" Peter asked, wishing he could pinpoint the location of their former homes and possibly get a lead as to where to find the monsters who were working for Henderson.

"From what we could ascertain, Brad was taken from Central Illinois and Dan from Minnesota. They were two and three at the time of their abductions. The journal says that both of the boys had been in the foster-care system. I have a feeling a lot of the kids they brought here were also in foster care."

Peter wracked his brain to try to understand where these boys were taken from. Since he got back to his studies just a few days ago, he'd been studying geography but still had no idea where Illinois or Minnesota was located within the United States. "I'm not familiar with either of those places."

Radon put his hand on Peter's shoulder. "You've progressed so quickly with your studies, I tend to forget there are still gaps remaining in your educational background. Those are states in the upper Midwest. Since you were taken from Missouri, Jake from Iowa and now these last two boys we're looking into from Illinois and Minnesota, that means they are more familiar with the Midwest than other parts of the country. With this information, they should be easy to find. Cassion has already alerted the St. Louis, Chicago and Minneapolis complexes. We don't have pictures of them, but Henderson kept good records, including fingerprints."

"Is it possible that Brad was abused by the man who kidnapped him?" Peter inquired.

"It's highly unlikely," Cassion replied. "According to the records, Brad was three at the time and in good health. Reading further, we learned that all of the sexual abuse was at the hands of Mrs. Henderson. Mr. Henderson was the one who administered the physical abuse."

Peter realized he had a lot to digest. Ever since he told the story of how his father kidnapped him and allowed Delos to bring him to the ranch, he'd avoided talking to Rawlins family. This morning he'd been told that Zander was awake. He felt as though he needed to bare his soul to the young man who tried to destroy everything they were trying to build on the property where his brother lost his life.

~ * ~

"I must caution you," Dr. Gratan began, "although your son is awake, he does tire easily."

Patsy Rawlins dabbed at the tears running down her cheek with the tissue Nurse Kara handed her.

"Can he talk to us?" Vern asked.

"He can, but he might not make much sense for a couple of days. He's been in the induced coma for over two weeks. During that time, he's done a lot of healing, but don't be surprised if he doesn't remember the reason he's in the hospital."

Although Josie wanted to go in and visit her brother, she agreed it was best if her parents went into the ICU unit first.

Patsy steeled herself for what they might find. They'd seen the healing for themselves during their visits to the hospital. Her biggest fear was that her son wouldn't know who they were. That would tear at her heart more than anything else.

"Mom, Dad, what are you doing here? Did I get the bastards who took Jake away from us?"

It came as a relief when Zander recognized them. Even more amazing was the fact he understood he was on the ranch where his younger brother lost his life.

"The person who took our Jake has been dead for over twenty years," Vern said. "As for the Hendersons, they've been tried and convicted for the crimes they perpetuated on this ranch."

"Then who are the bastards who are running this place? No one should..."

It was as though Zander's strength had suddenly been drained from his body. He'd slipped back to sleep, midsentence. "Is he...?" Patsy questioned.

"No, Mrs. Rawlins," Kara assured her. "Dr. Gratan told you his strength isn't back to what it should be. It's a good sign that he was able to recognize you and is aware of where he is. What he has to come to grips with is the crimes he's committed against Resurrection Ranch."

Kara calling Zander's actions crimes tore at Patsy's heart. Ever since they'd learned what happened to Jake, vengeance was all that Vern and Zander could talk about. 'Righteous justice' was what they called it. She doubted if either of them considered what they were planning to be crimes.

"W-what will happen to my son?" she managed to ask.

"That's not up to me to say. You would have to talk to my husband as well as Cassion about that. Mark is the manager of the ranch and it would be within his rights to press charges. Cassion, on the other hand, is more level headed. I know they've been working closely in the office to unearth the secrets this place has been harboring all these years."

~ * ~

By the time Peter came to grips with the atrocities perpetuated by the first boys raised at Henderson Ranch, instead of going out with the men, he made his way to the dining hall. There would be time for work later in the afternoon.

Across the room, he saw the Rawlins family seated at one of the more secluded tables. Although he wanted to go over to talk to them, he refrained. He needed more time to come to grips with what he'd learned over the past few hours.

After filling his plate, he started walking toward the table where Jerilyn and Hodia were seated when Josie Rawlins stopped him.

"Mom and Dad asked me to come over to see if you would eat lunch with us."

The last thing he wanted was to eat lunch with the Rawlins family. He also didn't want to be rude to Jake's sister and parents. Before following Josie to their table, he glanced over at Jerilyn. As though she understood what was going on, she nodded and smiled knowingly.

"Thank you for joining us," Patsy said. "Our son regained consciousness this morning. Up until now, we were only concerned with his recuperation. Do you think there will be criminal charges filed?"

Peter felt as though he'd been blindsided. As much as he wanted to shout, *Of course, he'll be charged. He stole cattle from us and burned down one of our barns.* Instead, he shook his head. "I'm not the person to ask. You must know I'm only the foreman here. Mark is the ranch manager and the property is owned by the people from the Cheyenne reservation in Montana. Those decisions are theirs to make."

"I was hopeful," Patsy said.

"He didn't do anything wrong," Vern adamantly stated. "This ranch took our boy away from us and killed him. We deserve revenge."

"The people you deserve revenge against are incarcerated for the rest of their lives. Also, the man who stole your son was murdered over twenty years ago. The people who own this ranch bought it from the state in order to give guys like my friends Chris, Mark, myself and the others a chance at a new life. If the truth be told, your son was one of the lucky ones. Many times, I wished I would have died before I had to endure the hell my life was before I was rescued. You say you want vengeance. Well, I want to learn to get past the nightmares. To get past memories of this." He pushed up his sleeve so his brand was visible. "Be glad your son never had to endure being sold to one of the slave ranches and being branded like one of the cattle. Be glad he wasn't starved and still expected to work a full day in the hot sun."

Peter hardly realized that his voice had risen dramatically. Suddenly, he could no longer control the tremors that overcame his body. Without warning, a black cloud descended, taking him to the bliss of unconsciousness.

~ * ~

Jerilyn could hear the hysteria in Peter's voice. Before she could get to him, he was on his feet, shaking uncontrollably before he slumped onto the floor unconscious. She rushed to his side, only to be held back by Hodia as Dr. Gratan, Kara and Radon surrounded him.

Within what seemed like hours, but in reality, was only minutes, two nurses from the hospital arrived with a gurney. She watched as Dr. Gratan and Radon lifted Peter to the gurney. They were followed out of the dining hall by Chris, Mark and Cassion.

"I want to be with him," she said, her voice hardly more than a whisper.

"I know you do," Hodia said, consolingly. "He's in good hands. You have to realize how hard all of this has been on everyone, but especially on Peter, Mark and Chris. They had the load of leadership placed on their shoulders. To be truthful, I've been worried that something like this might happen to one of them. I thought it might be Mark, but I do understand that Peter is dealing with a lot of nasty demons from the past."

Jerilyn nodded. Hodia was right. She'd been so busy with the younger children, there hadn't been time for her to start counseling with Peter and the others. She replayed the confrontation between Vern Rawlins and Peter. She'd been horrified when she saw Peter push up his sleeve and show them the brand that marked him as a slave, bought and paid for. If she knew anything, it was that he didn't show the brand to just anyone, especially not strangers. Perhaps that was what predicated his collapse.

"Before we go over to the hospital, why don't you contact Peter's mother," Hodia suggested. "She'll want to be here. Thank the One God that she's close enough to get here quickly."

Jerilyn agreed. Peter needed his friends and his family at this point. Later he would need her, but not now.

It took only a moment for Rita Hodges' face to fill the screen.

"Mrs. Hodges, this is Jerilyn, Peter's friend. He collapsed in the dining hall. I think it would be good for you to come to the hospital."

"Of course, I'll be there as soon as I can."

Relieved she'd done the right thing by contacting Peter's mother, Jerilyn followed Hodia's lead and took her tray back to the kitchen to clean off her dirty dishes. With that done, she went over to the hospital.

In the waiting room of the Emergency Department, she joined Chris and Mark, to wait for any news about Peter's condition.

"Why did the Rawlins want Peter to join them for lunch?" Mark asked, running his fingers through his hair.

"Unfortunately, I couldn't hear what they were saying," Jerilyn confessed. "I did see him push up his sleeve and show them his brand. Something must have been said to make him do that. On the first night we met, he showed it to me, but said he doesn't show it to many other people."

"I can attest to that," Chris said. "I remember it took several weeks before he trusted Mark and me to see it. He's got some deep-seated memories about the time he spent on that slave ranch. It's possible he put voice to what we've all been thinking. Jake was lucky to have died and not have to endure what we did over the years. I didn't suffer as much as the others did, but it was still rough."

Jerilyn nodded. "I know, he's said the same thing to me. I didn't think he actually meant it, considering he'd been rescued and reunited with his family. Apparently, it bothers him more than he let on."

"I feel the same way," Mark said. "I know I'm blessed to have been rescued and reunited with my family. It doesn't mean that the memories or the nightmares go away. If I thought my experiences in Mexico were horrible, from what I've heard from Peter, his were far worse."

Before they could continue further with their conversation, Kara joined them.

"How's Peter?" Mark asked as soon as she entered the room.

"He'll be all right, but Dr. Gratan wants to admit him to the hospital at least overnight so he can get some rest. As we all know, since his rescue, he's had very little time for rest. Between his studies, helping out with meeting the survivors we've brought here, and finding his family, he's been under more stress than any of us can even imagine. He's asking to see you, Jerilyn."

She got to her feet, just as Rita and Randy Hodges entered the waiting room. "I understand he asked for me, but his mother deserves to go in and see him first."

~ * ~

As consciousness returned, Peter felt humiliated at collapsing and having to be brought to the hospital.

"I've got work to do," he protested. "I don't have time to be here."

"I've been checking your records, and unlike many of the others, you've never had a complete medical examination," Dr. Gratan said.

"What about when I was hospitalized in Mexico City? Weren't those records transferred here?"

"They were. I've gone over them. In Mexico City you were stabilized. Before a complete examination could be conducted, Radon took you to Nevada for the trial for the Grangers. You are well aware of how busy you've been since then. Everything you've done has been for the good of Resurrection Ranch, not for the good of you. Your collapse today has given me the opportunity to give you a complete physical. It also gives you an excuse to get some rest. I realize your nightmares have robbed you of the rest you need. I plan to give you a mild sedative that will allow you to sleep peacefully. I predict it will do you a world of good."

"When you put it that way, Doc, I guess I don't have a choice in the matter. Do you think it would be possible for me to see Jerilyn before you knock me out or start your tests?"

"I think that could be arranged."

Dr. Gratan turned to Kara. "Would you go out to the waiting room and have Jerilyn come back?"

Peter watched Kara leave the room. He definitely wanted to talk to Jerilyn and perhaps make sense of everything that was going on. Almost as soon as she left, he saw the curtain partitioning his cubical from the others in the emergency room open. He was surprised to see his mother and Randy enter the small room.

"H-how did you know?" he stammered.

"Jerilyn called us. She was getting ready to come back to see you when we arrived. She thought it was best if we come back first. It's a mother's place to be by the side of her child."

Peter laughed at her logic. He'd read enough about the love between a parent and a child he realized his mother wanted to theoretically kiss his hurt away. "I'm glad you're here, but as you can see, I don't have any boo-boos for you to kiss away."

"Well, that's one way to put it," Randy replied. "To your mother you're still that little three-year-old boy who disappeared without a trace all those years ago. Since we've always known about you, we all understand her need to be by your side, not only today but for the rest of your life."

"Yes, I guess my husband is right. I'm grateful to Jerilyn for contacting me about your collapse. We just want to be certain you're all right."

"What about the girls? You didn't leave them alone, did you?"

His mother's expression was one of disbelief at Peter's question. "Good heavens, no. As you know, they're attending school with Terri and Buck, right here at the ranch. We will be taking them home with us once they're dismissed for the day. Of course, I doubt they'll want to leave before they make certain you're being well cared for. They're very protective of their big brother now that they've finally met you."

Although Peter was pleased with the concern of his family, he much preferred riding with the men to being the center of everyone's attention.

~ * ~

Jerilyn nervously paced the waiting room. She wished she'd been the first one to go to Peter's side, but she knew she did the best thing in letting his parents go in ahead of her.

Out of the corner of her eye, she saw the Rawlins family enter the area. In the back of her mind, she blamed them for Peter's collapse, even though she knew their discussion was merely the catalyst for what was bound to happen, sooner or later. Peter, like most of the survivors of Henderson Ranch, was plagued with demons of what they'd endured all through their childhood and young adult years.

"How is the young man?" Vern asked.

Mark and Chris got to their feet and held out their hands in greeting to Vern. "Peter is being admitted to the hospital for tests and observation," Mark said.

"What he told us, was there any truth in it?"

"I'm not certain what your discussion was about," Chris said. "I can only imagine that he told you your son was one of the lucky ones. He didn't have to endure being sold as a slave to one of the ranches in Mexico like Peter, Mark, Clint, Parker and Roger. Of course, Jerry, Ken, Dennis and myself endured a different kind of hell when we were with the skinheads. I was told he showed you the brand on his arm. That has to tell you what your son avoided by dying so young. I don't condone anything the Hendersons did to us, but there are times I wish I would have died."

"Until I saw the brand, I didn't want to believe those terrible things happened to any of you. I wanted revenge for the death of my son. I wanted to hate this place and everyone who lived and worked on it. I knew Zander felt the same way as I did. I encouraged him to seek the revenge I knew I was too old to do."

"If you're asking us for forgiveness," Mark began, "that's something we'll have to take under consideration. We've lost several head of cattle to say nothing of the barn that was burned and the men who were injured fighting the fire."

"Does that mean you're going to press charges against my brother?" Josie inquired.

"That's something else we're considering. My mentor, Cassion, is against pressing charges, but I'm not so sure. We've had several discussions about it. I doubt any decisions will be made until we have a security officer on our payroll."

"Payroll?" Patsy questioned. "Are you saying all the people who are working here are being paid?"

Chris laughed at her questions. "Of course, they are. Peter, Mark and I all have family living around here. That being said, we all have inheritances that more than pays for our needs. The others, including our teachers, medical personnel, ranch hands and chefs receive a salary. We plan to make this a superior seat of education as well as a self-sustaining cattle and horse ranch. Like a phoenix rising from the ashes, Resurrection Ranch is going to be reinvented into something to bring pride to everyone who lives and works here."

Jerilyn silently applauded both Chris and Mark for the way they handled the questions posed by the Rawlins family.

"Peter wants to see you before he goes up to his room. Jerilyn," Rita said when she entered the waiting area. "I want to thank you for allowing us to go in to see him first."

Jerilyn turned away from the conversation between the Rawlins family and her friends. "It was only fitting. Are you planning to stay on the ranch tonight?"

"No, we're close enough to go back home. That way the girls will be able to sleep in their own beds tonight. We'll be back in the morning when we drop the girls off at school. We know he's in good hands. We will stop back with the girls before we leave for the day. By that time, he should be settled into his room."

Jerilyn nodded in agreement. After bidding Peter's parents goodbye, she went back to where Peter was being readied to go up to a room.

"Do you have any pull with Dr. Gratan?" Peter asked when she entered the cubicle.

"You know I don't. Why do you ask?"

"He wants to admit me to the hospital for a complete physical examination. I don't have time to do anything like that."

"The way it sounds you don't have much choice in the matter. If you don't do what Dr. Gratan asks, I have a feeling Mark and Chris will be on your case about it. They've both undergone complete physicals as have most of the others. It's not going to do you any good to protest. From what I can see you're wound tight and need to relax. Nothing will fall apart if you have to take some time for yourself."

"I'm the foreman of this ranch. I'm needed."

"You're right, you are the foreman, but you have good men working for you. You tend to forget, I've interviewed all of the former residents and you can trust them to do a good job, be you there with them or not. Don't worry, none of them want to take over your position. They need you to be healthy and able to make the decisions they need made."

"You're as bad as the rest of them. Okay, I'll do what you all want. Everyone thinks there is a need for me to have this time to relax. I'm certain Dr. Gratan will find nothing other than I'm still suffering the effects of what happened to me both here and in Mexico."

~ * ~

Chris and Mark returned to the office. It bothered them that Peter was so reluctant to undergo the physical examination that each of them went through willingly.

"Do you think Peter has something to hide?" Chris asked.

"Don't we all? Have you disclosed everything that happened to you here on the ranch to say nothing of the skinhead group? Were your days with them all fun and roses?"

"You know they weren't. The indoctrination was rough. We were put through grueling exercises and forced marches along with the daily classes on hating anyone who was different."

"What would have happened if they found out about your Native American heritage?"

Memories flooded Chris' mind. In them he saw a young man who had begun indoctrination, only to admit he had an African American bloodline. He'd been singled out, made to strip naked, kneel on the ground in front of everyone, and was shot in the head because he wasn't completely white. *At the time I didn't know about my background. I thought the guy was a fool for admitting to something that wasn't obvious. I hated him like the rest of them. It haunts me day and night.*

"What about you? Are there things you haven't admitted to from your past?"

Chris watched as his friend slowly nodded his head. "While I was in Mexico, my owner used me, the way he would use a woman. It was horrible. When I cried and said it wasn't right, he had me beaten within an inch of my life. I never questioned anything that was done to me again. After that I saw one of the men I called my friend lose his life, because he refused our owner. We both know that life is a fragile thing. We've seen things that we should have never witnessed. We all have secrets. I just hope the ones Peter carries won't destroy him completely."

"The others who were rescued from that ranch seem to be well adjusted. Do you think we should have them checked out as well?"

Mark shook his head. "They were at the complex in Mexico City longer than Peter was. He did a lot of traveling after he was rescued. They were given the complete physicals and advanced counseling that Peter didn't receive. It's time we make certain he's stable."

Chapter Nineteen

Radon was worried about Peter. He cursed himself for not insisting on a complete physical examination before taking him to the trial in Nevada and to Canada to reunite with his family. He'd been negligent in his obligation where Peter was concerned.

He'd been worried about meeting with his superior ever since Cassion requested it shortly after Peter's collapse.

"You look like you're getting ready to face a firing squad," Cassion greeted him when he entered the room.

"Don't I have reason? Peter's collapse was my fault. With my educational background I should have insisted Peter have a complete physical before we went to Nevada or to Canada."

"Don't beat yourself up," Cassion consoled. "As far as any of us were concerned, Peter seemed to be the most well-adjusted of all of the survivors. From his records I can see he was given the best rehab help available while he was in Mexico City. As I recall, Mark had problems that we didn't find until several physical examinations were performed both in Denver and Nevada. I've talked to Gratan and he doesn't think he will find anything other than exhaustion and stress. This whole matter of what Zander Rawlins did to this ranch has to be weighing heavily on his mind. Even if he didn't recognize Jake's picture, he finally remembered him as being one of the older boys who taught him how to rope a steer. It's my opinion it's the stress of everything that is going on that has brought on his collapse. You have nothing to be worried about. You've done good things for Peter and everyone who matters knows it. I suggest you take your own advice and get some rest before you end up in the same shape as Peter."

Radon breathed a sigh of relief. He was positive Cassion would hold him as responsible for Peter's collapse as he held himself. To be absolved of his guilt was as though the One God had personally forgiven him for his negligence in regard to Peter.

~ * ~

After three days of tests and examinations, Peter was released from the hospital. Other than being anemic from the years of insufficient nutrition, he was proclaimed healthy. He had to agree the rest did him a world of good.

Before returning to his apartment, he decided to visit Zander Rawlins and find out what drove the young man to try to destroy Resurrection Ranch.

He didn't know how he would react to the young man. Dr. Gratan told him of the number of burns Zander had suffered. Would he be unrecognizable?

Peter laughed at the question that came to mind. He wouldn't have recognized Zander even without the burns.

As soon as he walked into the room, the man in the bed was suddenly an older Jake Rawlins. Had the rest Dr. Gratan insisted he needed jogged his memory? He blinked several times and the vision of Jake was gone. Instead, an older man, perhaps in his early thirties, faced him.

"Are you one of 'them'?" the man asked.

"Like your brother, I was kidnapped and brought here by Delos Reynolds. I grew up here. My name is Peter Solomon-Hodges and my father killed Reynolds so he wouldn't have to share the money Henderson paid for me."

"Did you know my brother?"

"We weren't allowed to associate with kids who were either older or younger than ourselves. I knew Jake, only because he was the one who taught me how to rope a steer. Otherwise, I had little to do with him on an everyday basis."

"I see."

"Why did you rustle our steers and burn down one of our barns?"

"Isn't it obvious? This ranch should have never been allowed to continue to exist. Someone should have destroyed it long before this. Up until now, I'm the only one who had the balls to do what needed to be done."

"Who told you it should be destroyed?"

"My old man and I have been talking about this ever since we were told what happened to Jake. Dear old dad said he was too old to do anything about it. It was my duty to carry out the plans we were making."

Peter could hardly believe what he was hearing. "Why would you hold the survivors of this hellhole guilty of what was done to us? I've often thought the kids who died in the box were the lucky ones. They didn't have to endure the torture of a lot of us who were sold to the ranches in Mexico. Three of the men who were with me in Mexico were close friends with your brother. They were the ones who recognized your picture. They're here for the same reason as I am. We want to get our lives back along with the education we were denied. My friends, Mark and Chris are behind the idea of having this ranch for those of us who need rehabilitation along with education."

"I've been watching this place. You have little kids here. Where did you kidnap them from?"

"They were kidnapped from the upper Midwest, but it wasn't by us. They were sold to Henderson, just like Jake and I were. We're giving them a chance at a good life. Even as young as they are, one of them wants to become a chef. Knowing that, we are gearing his educational program to prepare him for the future he's looking forward to living."

"I didn't know. We just wanted revenge."

"What are you doing in here?"

Peter turned to see Vern Rawlins standing behind him.

"I wanted to meet your son before I left the hospital. We've been getting better acquainted, haven't we, Zander?"

"That's right, Dad. Peter and I were clearing the air about what happened."

"I have to be leaving now," Peter said. "I'll be stopping back to see you again before your discharged."

Without a word to Vern, Peter turned and left the room. He had more information than he thought he would glean by talking to Zander. For now, he needed to talk to Mark, Chris, Cassion and Radon. Zander was as much of a victim as the rest of them. The difference was that his abuser wasn't Henderson—it was his own father who filled his head with hate.

It wasn't hard for him to envision how Vern Rawlins had poisoned his son's mind against Resurrection Ranch and the good they were hoping to do here. He'd listened to and believed Henderson for most of his life when he insisted Peter's mother was a dirty whore. Brainwashing was what Radon called it. Tell someone something enough times and they tend to believe every word of it.

It didn't take long for Peter to walk across the dooryard to the office. He was pleased to see Mark sitting at his desk.

"Hey, Buddy, I heard Dr. Gratan was springing you today," Mark greeted him. "How are you doing?"

"Other than being anemic, better than I was a couple of days ago. Do you think you can contact Chris, Cassion and Radon?"

"Sure, what's up? I thought once you were out of the hospital, you'd be on the back of your horse riding with the men."

"I would be, but I've gotten some information on what's been going on around here. It's something we all need to discuss."

"Sounds serious. Make yourself comfortable while I get in touch with the others."

Peter seated himself on the couch, when Anna entered the room. Even though she was Mark's paternal grandmother, she'd become important to all of the young men on the ranch.

"Peter, it's good to see you up and around. You gave us all a scare the other day. I've got Mark's snack, is there anything I can get for you?"

"No, thank you. I'm good until lunch is served. Have you taken over Mark's snack duty?"

"I have and it's my privilege to do so. I missed so much of my grandchildren's lives, it's the least I can do."

"They'll be here in about fifteen minutes. Chris is in class but Cassion said he'd get him excused, since this sounds serious," Mark said.

"Class," Peter repeated. "I didn't give that a thought. Shouldn't you be in class? For that matter, shouldn't I be in class?"

"Calm down, cowboy. My classes aren't until this afternoon and yours have been put on hold until you were up and about again. The way you sounded when you first got here, I think what is on your mind is worth interrupting Chris' class."

Mark no more than spoke the words than Chris, Radon and Cassion entered the office.

Once everyone was seated, Peter took a deep breath. "Before I left the hospital, I met and talked to Zander Rawlins. I was wondering what you are planning to do with him."

"We haven't turned this over to the authorities, if that's what you're getting at," Cassion said. "Why do you ask?"

"I don't think Zander is the person behind all of this. Remember when you told me that I'd been brainwashed by Henderson, Radon?"

"I do, but what are you getting at?"

"Zander was adamant about the need to destroy this ranch, but I doubt it's his idea. I think his father is so wracked with grief over what happened to Jake, he's poisoned the mind of his oldest son. It would do Zander a world of good to talk to Clint, Parker and Roger, since they were the ones who knew Jake the best. When I assured him that things were different now than when Henderson ran this place, he wanted to know about the little kids that were here. He thought we were going to torture them. I doubt these thoughts are ones that he had on his own."

"I agree with you," Radon said. "I've talked to Vern Rawlins and although he puts on a good front, I can see the anger that's seething just below the surface. I have a feeling he's been blaming everyone within earshot for what happened to Jake."

"So," Chris began, "what do you think we should do about Zander and Vern?"

"From a legal standpoint," Cassion said, "Zander is guilty of rustling and arson. There needs to be punishment, but I think the burns he received have been punishment enough. As for Vern, I would like to talk to Dr. Gratan about this. The man most definitely needs a complete mental and physical examination for us to understand what's going on. He needs medical help more than punishment. The problem is, we have no idea what they've done with our cattle. Until we find out and hopefully get our stock back, there's not much we can do."

"That brings up something I forgot to mention. I heard from Jason Culver earlier this morning. He's interested in joining us here on the ranch. His wife is also excited about the move. Since he will be here by the end of next week, I suggest we wait until he arrives before we make any concrete decisions on things."

Cassion smiled. "I totally agree with you. I see things from the legal point of view. He can give us an opinion from the law enforcement end of things. In the meantime, I think I'll have a talk with Zander Rawlins. It's possible he will be receptive to telling me where he took our cattle. With luck, he won't have sold them yet."

Chapter Twenty

Zander waited until Peter was out of earshot before he addressed his father. "What do you have against these people?"

"The same things as you do. They killed Jake. I want my revenge and I will have it."

"That's what I'm getting at. We've talked about revenge ever since we were contacted about Jake's death, probably even before that when he disappeared. It isn't the land or the people who are working to make it a prosperous ranch, who did this to Jake. Those people have been tried and convicted. They'll never be able to abuse children again."

"Where is your family loyalty? What about what we owe to Jake? He lived a terrible life and…"

"…and nothing, Dad. You didn't hear what Peter told me."

"You're getting soft. What lies did he tell you?"

"They weren't lies. He told me the man who kidnapped Jake did the same thing to Peter. True, it was his father who kidnapped him, but it was Delos Reynolds who sold him to this hellhole. He got what was coming to him when Peter's dad murdered him. From what they've learned, there were several guys who were the first ones to be raised on this ranch and they were behind bringing kids here, right up until the end. I just hope they catch these guys and give them the punishment they deserve."

"We'll see. I don't trust any of these people any farther than I can throw them."

To Zander's relief, his father left the room. All the negative rhetoric he'd heard ever since the day Jake disappeared echoed in his mind. He could no more hold the people who'd cared for him since the fire responsible, than he could himself for his brother's disappearance and subsequent death at the hands of the Hendersons. He knew he had to talk to Peter or one of the other survivors and do it soon.

~ * ~

Patsy was more than relieved when Vern said he was going to the hospital to check on Zander. She knew she couldn't take much more of the hate he delighted in spouting about this ranch and the people who ran it.

She needed to talk to someone, and decided she would see if the counselor, Jerilyn, was available. When she contacted the younger woman via her communicator, she'd been offered an appointment this afternoon. With Vern gone for the remainder of the day, there would be nothing to stop her from keeping the scheduled meeting.

From what she'd learned, the therapy office was in the educational facility, that was only a short walk from the apartment where she and her family were staying.

"Are you going somewhere, Mom?" Josie asked.

"I'm going to see the therapist. I can't take much more of your father's negative attitude about this ranch. They've been nothing but good to us, regardless of the cattle Zander rustled and the fire he set. Don't get me wrong, I loved your brother, Jake, with all my heart, but when he disappeared and couldn't be found, I resigned myself to the fact he was dead. When we learned that he died at the hands of the monsters who ran this place in the past, I was angry, but I also knew he was at peace. I followed the trial for the Hendersons and was relieved to know they were given the harsh punishment they deserved."

"I agree with you completely, Mom," Josie replied. "Would you mind if I came with you? I'm sick of all this talk of hate and revenge as well. To be truthful, I've been talking to Melian, and she said with my background in education, there might be a place for me here at the ranch. Along with the three little boys who were rescued, there are three little girls who were taken from a pervert who was grooming them to become prostitutes. I know I could do good things here. Unfortunately, between Dad and Zander, I would probably be disowned for even wanting to help out."

"I don't see any problem with you coming with me. Together, maybe we can come up with some idea of how we can undo the terrible things that have been perpetuated by your father and your brother."

~ * ~

Clint was surprised when Peter asked him to come to the hospital and see Zander. "Why me?"

"Zander wants to know what his brother was like. You, Parker and Roger were the same age. That said, you three knew him better than any of the rest of us would."

"That makes sense. Do you think he's going to tell us how we can get our cattle back?"

"I hope so. I was about to ask him about it when his father came into the room. That man is so filled with hate, it's frightening. I wouldn't put anything past him, including selling our stock and pocketing the money. When it comes to Zander, I have a feeling he was as abused as we were, just in a different way. Vern Rawlins has nurtured hate in Zander ever since the day Jake went missing."

"Mental abuse, like when Henderson told us our mothers were all dirty whores. That was just as bad as the physical and sexual abuse we all suffered while we were here. I actually feel sorry for the guy. When do you think we can see him?"

"I talked to Dr. Gratan and he said he'd let us know when Vern left Zander's room. I certainly don't want another run in with that SOB anytime in the immediate future."

He no more than spoke the words, when his communicator indicated a message coming in from Dr. Gratan. With the 'all clear' message, they made their way to the hospital to talk to Zander.

~ * ~

Zander was relieved when his father left his hospital room. He'd grown up on the hatred for what happened to Jake. Even though it hadn't been his fault, he felt guilty for not staying with his little brother on the day he was kidnapped. Maybe if he'd been there, Jake wouldn't have been taken. Maybe being two years older than Jake, he could have fought off his kidnapper. His life was full of maybes, but it all boiled down to the fact that if he'd been there, he could have done little if not nothing and might have ended up being sold to Henderson along with his brother. For the first time in all the years since his brother's disappearance, he realized he wasn't responsible for what happened to him. It was nothing more than a product of his father's warped hatred. The hate had to end and it had to end with him.

"Are you up to some more company?" Peter said from the doorway to Zander's hospital room.

"As long as it's not my dad, I guess so."

"That's good. This is Clint Anders, he's the one who recognized you from the picture we got from the internet café."

"So, did you know my brother?"

A soft smile graced Clint's face. "We were best friends. There were four of us the same age, Parker, Roger and I were all good friends with Jake. I remember the day he went into the box. He was being punished because he talked back to Henderson. We were out with the herd and one of the steers got loose. Jake went to find him and Henderson blew a gasket. He said that Jake had no business leaving the herd when he was supposed to be in charge of them. Jake told him that the herd was in good hands with the rest of us and he went after the one that was lost. I've been learning about the One God and the story I like the most is the one about the lost sheep and how the shepherd left the ninety-nine to find the one that was lost."

Zander wasn't ashamed of the tears that flowed down his cheeks. He remembered the story Clint told him about the lost sheep, from Sunday School. His brother did the right thing and it cost him his life.

"Was Jake punished often?"

He watched as Clint pondered his answer. "When we were little, we all got paddled by Mrs. Henderson and I got sent to the box once, but I don't remember Jake ever going there. We used to tease him and say that he was Henderson's favorite. A lot of good that did him in the end."

"What happened when you turned eighteen?"

"We all turned eighteen within the same year, and for some reason Henderson sold us all to the same ranch where he sold Peter two years later. If Jake would have lived, he would have been sent there too. I thank the One God every day that Jake was spared that torture. He was too good to have to endure the life we did. Even if he had been sent there, he wouldn't have survived for as long as we did."

"How did you survive? Were you branded like Peter?"

"Of course, we were, but we don't like to think about it. As for how we survived, I don't know. We all wished to die on a daily basis. I guess the One God kept us alive so we could come to this ranch to help Peter and the others to make it into something good."

Zander swallowed hard. "I'm embarrassed to admit that I wanted to destroy it."

"You were brainwashed just like we were, only it was your dad who did it to you and not Henderson," Peter said. "What I'd like to know is what happened to our steers?"

"Dad wanted them sold, but I found a deserted ranch where I could keep them until we found a buyer. I made certain there was good grazing there and a steam to provide them with water. I've read that, with the right pasture land, steers can basically take care of themselves."

"Can you tell us where this is?"

"I can. It's about twenty miles from here. Once I'm able, I can draw you a map."

"How did you transport them?" Clint pressed.

"Dad found me one of the old solar-powered trucks with a big trailer. He had it delivered to the ranch and I picked it up before I came here. Once I unloaded the steers, I left the truck there and flew to Las Vegas in my personal hovercraft."

"What I don't understand," Peter began, "is how do you support yourself? I mean, how could you take time away from your job to not only rustle our steers but also taunt us about it before burning down our barn."

"I work for my dad in his insurance office. There was no problem in getting the time off to do what Dad and I have been talking about ever since Jake went missing. I know there will be consequences for my actions. I hope by getting back your stock, we can work something out. I certainly don't want to be sent to one of the alien penal colonies."

Zander wondered what answer he would receive from either Peter or Clint. He expected the worst and hoped for the best.

"We don't know," Peter said. "That will be up to our mentors. Even though we're working here, we're still advancing our educations. We depend on men like Cassion and Radon to make the decisions we haven't the education to make. The one thing we can do is plead your case and let them know you are as much a victim of all of this as we are."

Once Peter and Clint left the room, Zander drifted off into one of the most peaceful sleeps he'd experienced since the day Jake went missing twenty years earlier.

~ * ~

Jerilyn reviewed her appointments for the day. With the starting of the school year, she'd had a long session with Brad. Although she thought she was making progress with him, starting back to the structure of the classroom seemed to send him into a tailspin.

Earlier, she'd received a communication from Diane saying Brad suffered a meltdown at the beginning of this morning's class.

Her session with Brad had been draining, but he equated Diane with Mrs. Henderson, since she lived in the main house. He was afraid she would punish him in the same way as Mrs. Henderson had when he disobeyed her.

It took over an hour but finally, she convinced him the punishments he'd experienced in the past were just that, in the past. Over the lunch hour, she'd accompanied Brad over to the dining hall where they shared the meal with Diane. By the end of the meal, Brad had calmed down considerably and he was able to return to his class. Since she'd heard nothing more from Diane, she was relieved and prayed there would be no repeat of this morning's meltdown.

She'd been surprised when she heard from Patsy Rawlins, requesting an appointment. Ever since the tormentor of the ranch had been identified as Zander Rawlins, she'd wondered about the make-up of the family. It was true they had every reason to hate what this ranch represented, but she prayed once they were here, they would realize more good than bad was being accomplished now that the former residents returned to continue their education and work to rebuild Resurrection Ranch into something of which to be proud.

A silent alarm on her communicator alerted her to the fact Patsy had arrived for the appointment they set earlier in the day. Talking a deep breath, she prepared to go into the outer office and welcome the woman she had not met personally, but seen from afar.

She was surprised when Patsy was accompanied by her daughter. Jerilyn searched her mind to come up with the young woman's name. It took a moment, but she remembered it was Josie.

"It's good of you to accommodate me," Patsy said, extending her hand in friendship. "I hope you don't mind that I brought my daughter with me. We've both lived with my husband's hatred for far too long. It's time we get some counseling so that we can start a new life."

Jerilyn nodded. Ever since the Rawlins family had arrived at the ranch, she had more questions than answers where any of them were concerned.

"What can I help you with?" Jerilyn asked, once they were comfortably seated in the sitting area of her office.

Patsy seemed to be uncomfortable, even though she had been the one who initiated the request for this meeting.

"Let me explain what has been going on in our family," Josie began. "I was just a baby when Jake went missing, therefore I never knew him. I know of him because my father has harped on it every day since it happened. I found I wasn't as passionate about it as Dad and Zander were, because I have no memories of my brother. I learned to live with it, that is until we received word that Jake's remains had been found on this ranch. That seemed to reignite the fire of Dad's hatred. Every day, he told us how this place should be destroyed. I was able to ignore most of it, but

Zander took the brunt of it as he worked with Dad. Of course, Mom had no choice but to listen to him."

Jerilyn watched as Patsy nodded her head in agreement of what her daughter was saying.

"When Zander disappeared, I asked Vern where he'd gone and Vern said he'd sent him to Minneapolis for the insurance seminar for two weeks. I don't get involved in the business, so I took him at his word. I should have asked more questions, but I never thought Zander would have come to Nevada to do the terrible things he did. I'm tired of hearing about how we need to get revenge for what happened to Jake."

"Were you surprised when you learned that Jake died at the hands of the Hendersons?"

"I most certainly was. After Jake had been missing for over two weeks, I resigned myself to the fact that my youngest son was dead. I never expected to hear that he'd been sold to Mr. Henderson or that he suffered a terrible death. Hearing the stories of several of the young men I've met since we came here, I tend to agree with them. He was better off dying here rather than enduring the terrible treatment they received once they left. I can see the good they are doing here, but my husband can't let go of the past. As far as I'm concerned, I'm ready to move on, with or without my husband and my oldest son."

Jerilyn was almost overwhelmed by the information Patsy was imparting to her. In the past she'd worked with children and young adults, but this woman could easily be her mother. How could she counsel her effectively? It was be easy to suggest divorce, but would it be the right thing to do in this situation?

"How do you feel about what your mom is telling me, Josie?"

"I agree with Mom completely. I've been talking to Melian and Hodia about staying on here as a teacher. I've been doing training to become a teacher for the past few years. I know I'm young, but I was able to take advantage of accelerated classes in secondary school as well as being able to enter college earlier than most. I'm so ready to be away from all the negativity in my family."

"If you were to break ties with your husband, Patsy, what would your plans for the future be?"

"I honestly don't know. I've been working at a local restaurant ever since Josie went to school full time. My income helped to pay for her college education, since Vern didn't approve of her going on to school. If he had his way, she'd be a secretary in his insurance office. He's kept Zander under his thumb ever since he graduated from high school. I suggested he go to college, but Vern insisted he should take the insurance test and join him in the business. They do work well together, but Zander feeds off his father's hatred. I pray he will be able to change his mind after what happened to him, but I have my doubts. He's grown up feeding off every word my husband says to him."

"I'm glad you felt you could confide in me. If you're serious about leaving your husband, your restaurant experience could lead to a position for you here on the ranch. That said, it's best for you to think on this before you make any decision. From what I've heard there are some legalities that have to be discussed concerning both your son and your husband. I know they are waiting until we get a security officer before any charges are filed. It's possible something can be worked out for the good of all."

Jerilyn watched as the expression on Patsy's face changed from concern to contentment. She'd expected tears at the mention of ending her marriage. Instead, she saw a light of hope. There was no way in which she could begin to understand the life Patsy and Josie lived. Her one hope was that in the future, they would be able to adjust to a new life, far away from Vern and his negativity.

~ * ~

Patsy felt as though the weight of the world had lifted from her shoulders after meeting with Jerilyn. "Did what Jerilyn have to say help you?"

She watched as her daughter broke into a broad grin. "More than you'll ever know, Mom. Let's go back to the apartment and freshen up for tonight's dinner."

"You've got a good idea. Hopefully, we can sit somewhere away from your dad."

Although Patsy spoke the words, she knew finding a place to be away from Vern would be next to impossible. He always insisted they eat every meal together. She remembered when she started working at the restaurant. He was livid that she wouldn't be home to fix his noon meal. When he started stopping at the restaurant and distracting her from her work, she purposely prepared his midday meal and left it for him in the refrigeration unit. All he had to do was reheat it in the sonic oven. He wasn't happy about it and still continued to come to the restaurant, until her boss told Vern he wasn't welcome there when she was working. She'd endured the brunt of his anger. After a few days, he came to grips with the idea of her working and him not stopping in to check up on her activities.

Together she and Josie took the elevator to their fourth-floor apartment. Unfortunately, all of her happiness disappeared as soon as she entered the apartment.

"Where the hell have you two been?" Vern demanded as soon as they stepped over the threshold.

"We were just out for a walk, looking around at what this place has to offer," Josie replied.

"Like hell you were. I was looking for you."

"You must have looked in all the wrong places," Patsy added.

"Do you know what that little bastard told me?"

"Who?"

"You know who. That little bastard I used to call my son. I know he must have been fathered by someone other than me He's gone soft. Wants to give back the cattle we took off this ranch. Well, that will happen over my dead body."

"What are you saying, Dad?"

"I'm saying that Zander has been listening to those young men who are running this godforsaken place. He was talking to that son of a bitch, Peter, when I got to the hospital. That kid was filling his head with a lot of bunk and Zander was taking it all for gospel. He knows what this ranch did to our family and he doesn't care."

"He does care, Vern, but he knows Jake has been gone for many years. The people who are running this ranch today are doing good. It's time for all of us to let go of the past and to heal."

The words no more than left her mouth when Vern slapped her hard enough to send her reeling across the room and down to the floor. When Josie tried to reason with her father, he hit her with a closed fist.

Even though she was dazed, Patsy saw Vern pull a laser pistol from his luggage. She knew he had one for protection at home, but she never thought he would bring it with him when they came to Resurrection Ranch.

Before either she or Josie could get to their feet, he stormed out the door.

"We have to warn them," Josie groaned, as she seemed to hover between consciousness and awareness.

Patsy nodded and activated her communicator. The last person she'd contacted had been Jerilyn, so contacting her now seemed to be the easiest thing.

"What's wrong?" Jerilyn said, as soon as her face filled the screen.

"It's Vern. He just hit both of us and left with his laser pistol. You have to warn them."

"Do you need medical assistance?"

"I-I don't know."

"I'll send someone over right away and alert the others to what's going on."

Pasty nodded her agreement with what Jerilyn said. She couldn't force any more words to come out of her mouth, as her head seemed to spin and her vision blur. It had happened before when Vern hit her, but it had never been this bad. She glanced over at her daughter and realized she'd lost consciousness. It was up to Patsy to stay alert so she could allow entrance to the emergency personnel who would be coming to their assistance.

~ * ~

Peter spent the majority of the afternoon with Mark and Chris in Mark's office. He'd relayed the information he'd received from Zander earlier in the day and they discussed how they would handle the return of their cattle.

"Do you actually think he'll tell us where he stashed our stock?" Chris asked, when they left the office.

"I hope so. He seems to be genuinely sorry for his actions," Peter replied. "The way it sounds, he's been brainwashed by his father, just like we were by the Hendersons. Vern has been preaching hate for so many years, it's no wonder Zander acted on it."

Before anyone else could make comment, Peter's communicator indicated an incoming communication. When he activated the device, Jerilyn's worried expression filled the screen.

"What's wrong? I can see it in your face."

"You bet it's wrong. I had a meeting with Patsy and Josie Rawlins this afternoon. I won't go into that now. Patsy just contacted me and said Vern was waiting for them when they got back to the apartment. I've alerted the hospital to send emergency personnel over to help them as he hurt both of them. Worse than that is Patsy told me he left the apartment with a laser pistol. I thought I should let you know so you can warn the others."

Peter nodded, knowing the others had heard every word Jerilyn spoke. Before the communicator went dark, there was a commotion at the dining hall. Without saying one word, they took off on a dead run.

Pandemonium reigned supreme when they entered the dining hall. Vern was shouting obscenities at everyone and Roger lay bleeding on the floor. Peter immediately rushed Vern only to feel a searing pain burn through his arm. What happened after that was a complete blur to him.

~ * ~

Alerted to the emergency in the dining hall, Radon and Cassion dropped what they were doing to get there as quickly as they could. The chaos that greeted them was indescribable. Peter and Roger lay bleeding on the floor, while several of the other cowboys wrestled Vern to the floor and held him there.

"You bastards all deserve to die. You did this to my family. I want retribution. I'll kill everyone on this goddamned ranch if I get a chance. I'm told there are young boys and girls here. How much money did they cost you? Are you going to kill them like you killed my son?"

"I'd advise you to keep your mouth shut, Mr. Rawlins," Cassion said. "You will be taken into custody and we will contact the law enforcement people at the closest office to take over your imprisonment. Up until now, we haven't contacted them regarding your crimes against this ranch."

"My crimes," Vern shouted. "I haven't committed any crimes. That was my son's doing."

"He wouldn't have done any of this if you hadn't nurtured his hatred for all these years. He's making progress and coming to grips with the truth about Resurrection Ranch and the people who are working to make it a place for education of those who were denied it when they lived here as children."

"You're wrong, wrong I say. This is a hellhole and it should be obliterated from the face of the earth."

Medical personnel rushed into the building to begin treating the injured. It was Dr. Cassion who administered a sedative to Vern in order to render him unconscious.

Cassion turned his attention to Roger and to Peter. "How are they?"

"I'm afraid Roger was dead before he even hit the floor," Dr. Gratan said. "The laser hit him directly in the heart. Peter, on the other hand, has a non-life-threatening wound to his arm. We'll be readmitting him to the hospital. I also have a team over at the apartments to attend to Patsy and Josey Rawlins. He assaulted them before he headed over here. I'm certain the man is deranged."

"In light of what transpired here today, I feel we have no choice but to contact the authorities to take custody of Mr. Rawlins. As you well know, there is no place on the ranch secure enough to hold him."

Dr. Gratan nodded his approval as he moved on to be of assistance to others who had been slightly wounded in Vern's rampage.

~ * ~

Kara was thankful that her parents had not been able to get a flight back to the dark side of the moon. When she got the call about Patsy and Josie being assaulted, they were visiting her at the hospital. Since both of them were in the medical field, they were more than willing to accompany her to the apartments. At the same time, a notification came in about there being shots fired at the dining hall.

While other personnel, including Dr. Gratan, were dispatched to see what was going on, they were left to care for the Rawlins' women.

Once they arrived at the apartment that had been assigned to the Rawlins family, she was relieved to see the door was ajar. Hurrying inside, she was horrified at the sight that greeted her. Patsy and Josie were both lying on the floor, bruises already beginning to show on each of their faces. Added to that, Patsy's left wrist lay at an odd angle. It was evident she'd tried to brace herself when she fell and fractured it. She tended to Patsy, while her parents concentrated on Josie.

"Mrs. Rawlins, can you hear me?"

Patsy's eyes fluttered open although Kara could see the pain radiating from them.

"Y-yes, is my daughter all right?"

"Don't worry about her now. She's being well cared for. We'll need to get both of you back to the hospital. I heard my father put in a call for two gurneys to be brought to transport both of you."

"I-I don't need a gurney, I can walk," Patsy protested.

"I'm certain you can, but there could be additional injuries that we don't see. I'm certain you have a fractured wrist and that is just what I can see. Just let us do our job and take care of you."

Patsy closed her eyes. Kara was concerned that the pain was enough for the woman to possibly lose consciousness again. Reaching into her bag, she administered a shot of a pain reliever along with a sedative and waited until the orderlies arrived with the gurneys.

The pain reliever seemed to work almost instantly as Patsy drifted into a pain free sleep.

Kara turned her attention to her parents. "How is Josie doing?"

"Whoever hit her broke her jaw. She's going to have a long recuperation," her father advised. "I pray there will be no other injuries because of this man."

She completely agreed with her father, but from what Jerilyn told her, the man was armed and nursing his misplaced hatred. She'd heard it when he was in Zander's room earlier. Just from that memory, she knew this wasn't going to turn out for the best.

~ * ~

Mark entered the dining hall several steps behind Peter. The scene unfolding before him was terrifying. Roger lay lifeless on the floor and Peter was confronting Vern. There was no time for any action as the flash from the laser pistol was blinding. Seeing Peter reel away from Vern with blood running from where he was wounded, prompted Mark into action.

He wasn't alone when he rushed Vern, knocking the pistol from the man's hand and pinning him to the floor.

Mark could hear the moans of others and realized there were more injured than just Roger and Peter.

How could this happen here? Resurrection Ranch was meant to be a place for healing, not the horrific injuries this man has inflicted on everyone here.

Dr. Gratan and his team seemed to miraculously appear to administer medical assistance to the injured. As much as Mark wanted to concentrate on what was being done for his friends, he couldn't let go of the man responsible for the carnage all around him in the dining hall.

At last, Cassion took control of the situation. Where he got the electronic cuffs he put on Vern's wrists was a mystery to Mark. He was relieved to no longer have to restrain the man who had been ranting ever since they'd tackled him.

With Mark no longer responsible for Vern, he turned his attention to Peter. He could tell by the look on his friend's face that he was going into shock. Thankfully, he was being given the necessary medical attention.

Hearing that Roger was dead was like a knife had stabbed Mark in the heart. To have survived the hell of living on Henderson Ranch as well as one of the slave ranches in Mexico only to be killed by a madman in the one place where he'd felt safe was beyond belief.

Across the room, Ken, Dennis and Jerry had shielded the children against not only the horrors of death but also for protection from the laser rays that had been shot into the room.

"How many were injured?" he finally managed to ask.

"Two of the cowboys," Clint replied. "Parker was also grazed and if I'm not mistaken, Jerry and Dennis were also grazed. It all happened so fast, none of us had time to react until it was too late. I can't believe Roger is dead. We were together in Mexico and he took a lot of punishments there. For him to die here while we were all trying to put our lives back on track is unbelievable."

Mark agreed. He wished he could turn back time and somehow be able to stop what happened here. Of course, he knew it wasn't possible. They'd have to find a way to overcome this and continue on with the work they came here to do.

Sirens seemed to scream from all directions outside of the dining hall. It was apparent someone had called the authorities to take custody of the man who was responsible for all of this. He turned to see uniformed officers enter the room.

Once Vern was taken into custody, detectives began taking statements from everyone who had been present when the carnage began.

Mark made his way to where Chris and Melian were comforting each other. He wished Kara was here, but he knew she was needed at the hospital. For the time being he needed to be his own comfort.

He saw Jerilyn enter the room and hurry to Peter's side. Mark was glad to see her as he knew she would be able to comfort and calm Peter.

If it hadn't been for her warning things could have been much worse than it was.

"You look like you need someone beside you," Terri said.

He wasn't aware of her being in the dining hall before he heard her voice. "Were you here when…"

"When this all happened? No, I wasn't. We were just getting home from school when everything happened. Mom wouldn't let us come in until we were told it was safe. I saw you over here all by yourself and Mom sent me over to bring you to where we are. She said you need your family now."

"My family," Mark mumbled.

It was still hard to believe in the meaning of family. At this moment, he knew he needed all of the members of his family more than ever before. Following Terri's lead, he headed over to the other side of the room where Diana, Buck, Anna and David were assembled.

Like a frightened child, he allowed Anna to take him in her arms and give him comfort. "How could this have happened?" he managed to say between muffled sobs.

"None of us knows why bad things happen to good people," he heard Pastor Joel say. "Perhaps it is the will of the One God that Vern gets the help he needs and taking Roger's life was part of the plan. None of us know how many minutes, hours, days, weeks or years we have been allotted. For us, it isn't fair and yet today Roger is with our Lord in Paradise."

Although Mark knew Joel's words were meant to be of comfort, he was hurting too much to accept them on face value.

~ * ~

Kara and her parents stayed with their patients all the way to the hospital. She blessed the thought that the main area of the ranch was so compact. It made getting Patsy and Josie to the emergency room for treatment as quickly as possible.

She was horrified when she saw the number of young men who were in the emergency area. "What has happened?" she asked one of the orderlies.

"Mr. Rawlins opened fire on the people in the dining hall. One of the young men is dead and there are several who are injured."

Kara's mind ran wild. She was supposed to meet Mark at the dining hall but had been delayed by the emergency with Patsy and Josie. What if Mark had been the one who was killed. How could she live without him, especially now that she knew she was carrying his child? She'd only confirmed her pregnancy this morning and was planning to tell Mark over the evening meal. What if he died not knowing he was going to be a father in a matter of months?

Once she was certain her patients were being well cared for, she made her way to check on the other victims of the shooting, praying all of their wounds would be minor.

She was shocked when she saw Peter in the first bed. He had a laser burn in his right arm and from the color of his complexion, she could tell he was in shock, either from the injury or from the loss of blood.

Turning away, she saw a shrouded figure being wheeled toward a private room. Fear mixed with gall that threatened erupt at any moment. What if the body under the shroud belonged to her husband? How would she handle it if…?

"Kara, thank the One God you're here."

She turned, relieved to see Mark coming toward her. Her emotions overwhelmed her as she rushed into his waiting arms. "I was so afraid. They told me someone had been killed and I saw them wheel in the body. I-I…"

"You were afraid it was me who got killed. I'm sorry you were so worried. I got to the dining hall after Rawlins killed Roger. We no more than entered the room when Peter got shot. Chris and I were the first to rush Rawlins. The others who weren't injured helped us to subdue him."

"I would have been there," Kara began, "but before all of this went down, he assaulted Patsy and Josie. I was at their apartment treating them. Patsy has a badly bruised face and a possible broken wrist. Josie has a broken jaw, at least that's what my father said. He and Mother went with me."

Mark pulled her into a tight embrace. She could tell he was hurting as much as any of the people who had been wounded in the confrontation with Rawlins. "Are you okay?" she asked, her voice hardly louder than a whisper.

"Yes, no, I don't know. It was horrible. So many people were injured and Roger was just lying there dead. This wasn't what I ever wanted for this place."

"I know, but we can't give up on Resurrection Ranch. We can't let Roger's death destroy what we've built already."

Kara and Mark turned at the words spoken by Chris. It was apparent he was as shaken as Mark, but his was the voice of reason.

"I realize I'm not in on the day-to-day workings of this ranch, but I am involved with the educational aspect. We planned to make a difference here and we have. Despite what happened here today, the ranch and the educational program will go on. What we have to worry about now are the people who were wounded as well as the publicity this will generate. For now, we have to prepare ourselves to meet with the law enforcement people and give our statements."

Kara watched as her husband's expression turned from despair to pensive as he thought over what Chris said.

"You're right," Mark began. "We can't abandon what we've begun because of one man's hate. Roger gave his life for this place and for that I grieve. I can assure you, he will not be forgotten by anyone here on the ranch. Let's go in and check on the guys who were injured."

Chapter Twenty-one

Within twenty-four hours of Vern's attack on Resurrection Ranch, the details of what occurred had spread worldwide. For Caroline it brought back memories of the mass shootings of the twentieth and twenty-first centuries. If she thought this was a more peaceful era, she was mistaken. Since coming out of her suspended animation, she'd seen the evil done by people like the Hendersons and the owners of the ranches in Mexico. She'd never expected to be in the midst of a mass shooting.

Out of concern for Vern's family and what they must be experiencing because of his actions, she took the elevator to the floor below hers and requested admission to their apartment. She was pleased when the door opened. Josie was reclining on the couch, while Patsy got to her feet in greeting.

"I'm Caroline Lewis-Phillips. We haven't formally met, but I was wondering how are the two of you doing?"

"I remember reading about you when they found you out in California," Patsy said, her eyes wide with either wonder or admiration. "I should be asking the same of you. What's it like being called the modern-day sleeping beauty?"

Caroline laughed. "I'm hardly that. To be truthful, I was little more than a coward. My husband had died in China of Covid-19 and I didn't want to get it. I went to sleep in one century and woke up in another. Of course, I didn't come here to talk about me. I'm afraid the publicity surrounding the events of the last few hours is going to be very hard on you."

"It could be, if I let it. Unfortunately, I realize all too well what my husband is capable of. If I'd known he brought his laser pistol I would have found a way to dispose of it. Now he's murdered an innocent man and injured many others. There is no way I can ever go home and face my friends. We live in a very small town and I'm certain word has already spread about what he's done. Even my son isn't innocent in this incident. Josie and I have decided to begin new lives, away from both of them."

"Don't be too hasty when it comes to your son. I've been talking with Chris. He's in charge of the educational department here. Before everything happened yesterday, he met with Mark and Peter. The three of them are convinced, without the influence of his father, your son would have never been involved in the rustling or the arson. They have decided to talk with the authorities about not pressing any charges against him."

"How can that be? He stole the cattle and set the fire."

"He also suffered severe burns in the process. Everyone feels he can be reeducated and since he's told them where to find the cattle, they feel he deserves a second chance. That's what this ranch is all about, second chances."

"I don't know what to say. I thought we'd lost him as well as Vern. How can we ever begin to repay such kindness?"

"I talked to Jerilyn and she told me you might be interested in staying on at the ranch. I've reviewed Josie's teaching credentials and I'm certain she would be an asset to our program. As things stand now, we are severely understaffed in that department. Also, your restaurant experience could be a boon to the chefs at the dining hall. There are only two of them and they're finding they're overwhelmed. They need to train someone to help with their duties and give them some time off."

"That's something we're going to have to think about. It sounds like the perfect solution and a way for us to make retribution for the damage our family has done."

~ * ~

Although Peter's injury was enough to sideline him for several days, he made his way to Zander's hospital room. Earlier, he'd made plans with Chris and Mark to meet with Zander and discuss what they'd decided where he was concerned.

"You're looking better than you did yesterday, Buddy," Chris greeted him.

"I'm not ready to go back to work, but luckily, Dr. Gratan was able to clean up the wound and stop the bleeding. He said I should be as good as new in a couple of weeks. I still can't believe we lost Roger and so many others were wounded. Roger was one of our best hands. I doubt we'll ever be able to replace him."

"I know what you mean," Mark agreed. "If it hadn't been for Dennis, Jerry and Ken, it was possible one of the children might have been injured. Unfortunately, Dennis and Jerry sustained minor injuries."

"That brings us to Zander," Peter said. "Under the circumstances, are we still in agreement to offer him a place here on the ranch to rebuild his life and not press charges against him?"

Peter's question went unanswered for several seconds. It was Mark who finally voiced his opinion. "I've had a long talk with Pastor Joel and he reminded me that the sins of the father shouldn't be held against the son. Like we said yesterday, he was brainwashed by his father. In other words, he's as much of a victim as we are. We agreed then, and I'm certain we still do, that he deserves a second chance as much as the rest of us."

Peter was relieved. After the talks he'd had with Zander, he saw him as a confused young man, who's mind had been poisoned with hate ever since his brother was kidnapped by Delos Reynolds.

"Since we're still in agreement, let's go in and talk to him," Chris suggested.

~ * ~

Zander pondered his future. His father was a monster who had killed someone and injured several others. Although his actions were not as damaging, he knew he was guilty of cattle rustling and arson. There would have to be retribution. He couldn't stand the idea of being incarcerated, yet he knew it was inevitable.

He was surprised when Chris, Mark and Peter entered his room. He immediately noticed Peter had his arm in a sling and could only imagine he'd sustained the injury at the hands of his father.

"How are you feeling?" Peter asked.

"Better than I should be. I've had great care here."

"We have something we need to talk to you about," Mark said.

Zander could feel his stomach begin to churn. The punishment for his actions was about to be pronounced and he didn't know if he was ready to hear the decision of these young men who only wanted to make a difference in the world.

It was Chris who pulled a chair up in order to pronounce the verdict.

"We've had a lot of discussion about this. At first, we wanted to prosecute you to the fullest, but we've gotten to know you. It's apparent you were abused, just as we were, although not in the same way. Your father nurtured his hatred onto you. If he hadn't, you would be a different person. Since we will be getting our cattle back and the barn is being rebuilt, we've decided you need another chance. What we're proposing is once you're healed, if you would be willing to make a new life here at Resurrection Ranch, we won't press charges. We can use your expertise in the insurance industry, but if you feel there are other fields you want to branch out in, we would be willing to offer you any education you want."

"I-I don't know what to say. What about my mother and my sister?"

"My wife and I met with your sister before what happened yesterday. She expressed a desire to join us in the educational department. Her credentials are excellent and I'm certain she would be an asset to our program. As for your mother, I'm certain there would be room for her here as well."

"What about my dad?"

"He's been arrested and is charged with murder and several counts of attempted murder," Mark replied. "Many of our people were injured. It's not something that can be excused. He can never give life back to Roger or make the wounds the others sustained go away. He is in the custody of the local sheriff and prosecuted to the letter of the law. Unfortunately, he may never serve a day in prison, since it's evident he's mentally unstable. If that's what is decided, we will do whatever we can to see that he gets the help he needs."

"How can you be so forgiving? We did terrible things to you."

"This ranch did terrible things to all of us," Peter said. "That's in the past. We are trying to build it up for the future. There are eleven of the survivors of this ranch who are ready to make those changes. It's not just those of us who aged out of the program, but also the children who were rescued and have had no parents to claim them."

"Peter's right," Chris commented. "The three of us were lucky enough to have found our families. In doing so, they have all become part of what we're trying to accomplish here. They've given us both financial and emotional support. Mark's family, more than the others, have become personally involved. His step-mother and half siblings are living here. While the kids are finishing their educations, Diane is teaching at the educational facility. His paternal grandmother is helping out wherever she can and his maternal uncle is going to build a veterinary practice here as well as overseeing a program for education in that field. That said, you're also lucky to have a mother and sister who are interested in helping us build something good here, in memory of not only Jake but all of the other kids who lost their lives under Henderson's watch."

Salty tears flowed from Zander's eyes, stinging his now healing skin. "I would be honored to do whatever I can to make amends for not only my actions but also those of my father. If you can forgive me, I can take this first step to change my life and help in any way I can."

Coming Soon
by the Author
at
Rogue Phoenix Press

Unknown in a New World
The New World Book Six

Prologue
Savannah, Georgia 1990

Anthony Montgomery couldn't believe his ears when he returned home from university. Sure, he'd done some crazy things, but he'd gotten his degree and was ready to take his place in the family business.

His father had been waiting for him to pull into the circular drive of their country home. From the look on his face, Anthony knew something was amiss.

"You're no longer welcome here," his father said, his voice laced with anger.

"What do you mean? I'm the oldest son, your heir."

"Like hell you are. Your mother admitted she was pregnant when we got married and I wasn't the father. She also admitted to several other affairs while we were married."

"When did she do that? She passed away several months ago. I was at the funeral and I didn't hear a word about anything like this."

His father shook his head. "How could you? I only found the letter confessing to her infidelities three weeks ago when I was going through her private papers. In them I found a letter she'd written when she found out about the cancer. She admitted to having an affair college student friend of hers. She also said that after they had sex, she realized she was pregnant and immediately had sex with me so I would marry her. To make matters worse, she told me, the bastard was from Wisconsin. A Yankee. She slept with a damn Yankee. She didn't even have the decency to have an affair with someone more acceptable."

"Then I could be your son."

"Hardly. Although I wanted to, she kept insisting we wait until we were married before we have sex. I thought I'd finally worn her down when she agreed to go to bed with me. Little did I know I was nothing more than a pawn and I would be raising another man's child."

"So, what am I to do? You're the only father I've ever known. I was going to take over the company. That's what I've been studying to do."

"Your younger brother will be taking over the company. As for you, I've packed up your things. They should fit in your car and I'll give you enough money to live on until you decide what to do with your life."

To say Anthony was in shock would have been a gross understatement. He watched as his father turned his back on him. The old man stood like one of the stone statues at school, while Anthony went into the house. Two boxes were waiting for him to take them out to his car.

On top of one of the boxes was thick manilla envelope. Opening it up, he found it full of family pictures, at least the ones of just him and his mother. None of the pictures showed his father or even his younger brother, Rick.

After packing the boxes in his car, he sought out his father. "I-I wanted to thank you for everything."

"No thanks needed. I've opened a bank account for you at Wells Fargo Bank. I checked and they have branch offices all over the United States. No matter where you end up you will have access to the money. All I ask is that you never contact me again. You can continue to use the last name of Montgomery. If you should ever step foot on this property, I will have you arrested and the money will no longer be at your disposal. I will not have Sherilyn's bastard claiming to be my son."

"Whatever you say, Gerald. I assume you don't want to have me call you Dad."

"You assume right. Just in case you want to call someone dad, try looking for your real father in Wisconsin. His name was Cam Rogers. At least that's what your mother wrote in that damnable letter of hers. I wanted to burn the thing, but I put it in with the photos of you and your mother. I wish you luck, but for now, I want you off this property as soon as possible."

Anthony nodded, still too shocked to say anything more. After getting into his car, he peeled out of the driveway, leaving behind the only life he'd ever known. He wondered what his father would tell their friends, neighbors and family about why he hadn't returned from college to take his rightful place at the head of the company.

Before leaving town, he drove past Montgomery Industries. He wanted one last look at the building that once represented his future.

"Well, I hope you enjoy running the company, Rick. The old man will blow a gasket, when he finds out you have no interest in Montgomery Industries or even having an heir for that matter. Just wait until he finds out about your boyfriend, Fred or is it George this month?"

His words were for his ears only. For a moment he wished he could stick around and see how everything turned out. Unfortunately, this city, as well as this state were no longer in his plans. Maybe in the future, he'd know what happened, but not now. For now, he was bound and determined to make his way North to Wisconsin and see if he could find Cam Rogers, whoever that might be.

It was almost dark, when he pulled into a roadside rest area to get some sleep. He'd stopped in the last town and purchased a burger and fries at a fast-food joint. At least they were still warm when he pulled them from the bag.

For the first time, he looked at the bank book his father had thrust in his hands before he left. It shocked him to see the balance was one hundred thousand dollars. If nothing else the old man paid him handsomely for leaving and giving up the life he expected to live.

Chapter One
Minter, Wisconsin 2021

Jayme Peters couldn't believe her eyes. Parked on the side of road just outside of town was the most beautiful 1990 Land Rover she's ever seen. Her dad ran classic car restoration company and would never believe she'd seen one of the first SUV's that was in such pristine condition.

Who in their right mind would leave this car in the middle of nowhere? Don't they know how much it's worth?

After making a U-Turn, she pulled up behind the abandoned vehicle. If nothing else, she could tell her dad she's seen the interior. If it was a pristine as the exterior, he'd be excited.

She was surprised when a young man got out of the car. He looked much too young to be driving an expensive antique vehicle.

"Hello," he said, his soft drawl signifying he wasn't from Wisconsin. "Can you tell me how much farther it is to Minter, Wisconsin?"

"You're just outside of town. How long have you been parked here?"

"I pulled off last night, when I was too tired to drive any further. I'm looking for someone, my dad."

This guy wasn't making any sense. She just drove past here a couple of hours ago and the car wasn't there.

"Are you sure about that?"

"Of course, I'm sure. Do you know Cam Rogers?"

"You're kidding, right?"

"Why would I kid about that? I have a letter from my mom. In it, she said in 1967 she had an affair with Cam Rogers and I was the product of that affair."

"That's impossible. That would make you fifty-four years old. There's no way you're any older than what twenty-two maybe twenty-five but that would be stretching it."

"Fifty-four? I'm twenty-three and I just graduated from college. Isn't it enough that my old man kicked me out because my mom confessed that I wasn't his son?"

Jayme did the math in her head. If this guy thought he was twenty-three years old and his mother had an affair with her grandfather in 1967, there was something definitely wrong.

"Are you okay to drive?" she asked.

"Of course, I am. I got a solid night's sleep. I'm getting used to sleeping sitting up."

"Good, why don't you follow me? Something tells me you could use a good meal. By the way, my name is Jayme Peters. Who are you?"

"Anthony Montgomery, but you can call me Tony."

~ * ~

Tony watched as Jayme walked back to her car. She wore the shortest shorts he'd ever seen and they hugged her body in ways that drove him wild. Even more interesting was the car she was driving. He'd never seen anything like it before. It was a little red sports car, but he couldn't identify it. Of course, he'd never been north of the state line before he took this road trip. Maybe they had different cars in the North than in Georgia.

She pulled out from where she'd parked behind him and he followed. Last night this road had been a bustling highway, now it seemed to be little more than a country road. Something was wrong, but he couldn't put his finger on it.

Minutes later, Jayme pulled into the driveway of what had once been a prosperous farm. Only now, it looked like there was no farming done here. There were crops in the field, but the barn hadn't been used in years. He decided what he'd learned in college was right, the little farmers were being forced out of business. He wondered if her family owned the acreage or if they just had the area around the house and the outbuildings.

"This is home. The farm belonged to my Grandpa Peters. He passed away about six years ago but he'd sold the cows years before that. He had Parkinson's Disease and couldn't do the work. My dad runs his shop out of one of the outbuildings and we rent out the land."

"Interesting. As I recall, you didn't tell me if you know Cam Rogers. Is he still living around here?"

Jayme hesitated before answering. "He lives in town. Mom can tell you more about him. I'm sure she has lunch ready."

"Lunch? What about breakfast?"

"Ah, it's noon. We had breakfast at seven this morning."

Noon? How could he have slept so long? It didn't matter, he was starving. He didn't care if it was bread and water, he needed something to eat.

As soon as he walked into the house, he was shocked. The kitchen looked like something he'd seen in a futuristic magazine. All of the appliances were stainless steel, the counters were of the finest garnet and there was a flat screen sitting on the counter. The open floor plan looked into the living room where the biggest black screen TV he ever saw was attached to the wall. He would have thought it was a picture of some kind, but there was a movie playing on it. He didn't know such things existed.

"Mom," Jayme called, "I found someone parked alongside the road. He seems to be confused so I brought him home. He's looking for Cam Rogers."

The woman who came into the room, wore a pair of shorts and a tank top. He would never envision his mother wearing something like that. She never even wore slacks, to say nothing of shorts.

"Welcome to our home. I'm Julie Peters and Cam Rogers is my dad. Why are you looking for him?"

"Because I was told he's, my dad. I don't understand any of this."

"I don't either, but let me fix you some lunch and we can sort this out. I hope you like BLT's."

Tony nodded. He'd eaten BLT's at one of the diners where he stopped on the way up to Wisconsin, but their cook would have never served sandwiches of any kind for lunch.

"Are you okay?" Jayme asked. "You look perplexed."

"I am. Nothing makes any sense. Your mom says she's Cam Roger's daughter, but she's old enough to be my mom. From what I was told, my mom and this guy had an affair when he was in college at the University of Georgia in 1966."

"My dad did go to the University of Georgia. He was drafted and went to Vietnam in January of 1967. When he came home in 1970, he married my mother and I was born a year later. He did finish his education at the University of Wisconsin Madison."

Tony put his hand on the counter to keep him upright when his knees threatened to buckle. If Julie Peters was Cam Roger's daughter, that would make her his sister. She should be nineteen, not old enough to had a daughter Jayme's age.

"There has to be a mistake. This is 1990…"

"Correction, this is 2021. I'm going to call my dad and get to the bottom of this."

"2021? How can that be? I left home a week ago in June of 1990."

Julie helped him to the recliner in the living room. "Do you believe in time travel?"

"That's science fiction."

"Maybe it is, but how else can you explain you being here thirty-one years after you left home? Somehow, you must have entered some kind of a time warp and been transported to the here and now. I'm going to call my dad and we can straighten this out. While we're waiting for him, I'll get you a sandwich and a glass of lemonade. It's warming up, and at least it's cool in here."

Tony tried to put everything into perspective. Time travel was alien to him, but it was the only explanation for all the strange things in this house.

He was surprised when Julie presented him with the sandwich on a paper plate, along with some potato chips, a radish, pickle spear and several carrots. Even the carrots were like nothing he'd ever seen before. They were miniature versions of full-sized carrots. How had they grown anything like that? He decided not to ask questions. The food looked too good to leave it sitting on his plate.

When he finished his sandwich as well as the relishes on the plate, Julie brought him a piece of pie that was unlike anything he'd ever eaten.

"I hope you like rhubarb pie," Julie said.

"I don't know. I've never had anything like it before."

"Do you drink coffee?"

Tony nodded because his mouth was full of the most delicious dessert he'd tasted in months. Reluctantly, he swallowed. "Black please."

As though Jayme was waiting for him to tell them how he liked his coffee, she entered the room with a mug of coffee in her hand. She went back into the kitchen and came out with her own paper plate holding the sandwich along with the relishes.

From the kitchen, Tony could hear Julie talking to someone on the phone. Was it possible she was calling the man who fathered both of them?

For some reason, Tony felt as though he couldn't hold his eyes open any longer. Cautiously, he leaned his lead back against the padded cushion of the chair. To his surprise, Jayme came and pushed his button on the side of the chair, making it recline.

He didn't have long to contemplate what was happening, as his eyes closed and he fell asleep.

~ * ~

"Do you believe him, Mom?" Jayme asked as they went out on the porch to wait for her grandfather to arrive.

"I don't know what to believe, but that vehicle he's driving looks like it's brand new. That along with some of the things he's saying makes me think there might be something to this time travel nonsense your brother keeps talking about. Before today, I just thought he was watching too many of those old Star Trek shows. Now, I'm not so certain."

Jayme watched as her grandfather pulled into the driveway. He always drove the newest and best vehicles. Just last week, he'd purchased a new Subaru. It was a cherry red convertible with a white interior and it suited him well.

"You didn't say much on the phone, Julie. What's so urgent? Does it have anything to do with that 1990 Land Rover in the driveway?"

"I'm afraid it does. Jayme found him parked by the side of the road. He asked her how far it was to Minter and if she knew you. When he got here, he told us he was looking for his father, you. I thought it was something he made up until he told me about his mother having a fling with you while she was in college at the University of Georgia. I know it sounds crazy, but somehow, he must have gone through some kind of a time warp. You know like what Tanner is always talking about."

Jayme watched as her grandfather seemed to be deep in thought. For a fleeting moment, she could see a resemblance between him and Tony. Damn it, the last thing she wanted was to realize Tony was her uncle, her mother's brother. He was so handsome, she could easily fall in love with him, but that would be incest.

~ * ~

Cam looked back at the Land Rover. As his son-in-law would say it was in cherry condition. He doubted if there was more than ten thousand miles on it. What Julie said was more science fiction than fact and yet, he remembered the night he told Sherilynn Graham that he'd been drafted and was probably going to Vietnam. One thing led to another and in the end, they'd made love. He hadn't thought of her in years, but it was entirely possible she'd gotten pregnant.

Afterward she cried. Although, he knew he wasn't her first she told him she was in love with Gerald Montgomery and hadn't allowed him to make love to her. She said she wanted her wedding night to be her first time with him. He understood completely. She was just someone he knew at college, not someone who he was ready to settle down with.

Before going into the house, he went to the vehicle and looked inside. It was, indeed, an expensive model. In the back he could see two cardboard boxes and a manilla envelope lay on the passenger's seat. The odometer read three thousand two hundred and fifteen miles. It was mind boggling. It made Julie's story of time travel almost believable.

"Has Don seen this car?" he asked when he returned to the porch.

"Not yet. He's gone to Madison for some parts for a car he got in last week. I don't expect him back until four or five this afternoon."

"I guess it's time I got to meet this young man."

~ * ~

Tony woke slowly. It was as though he sensed someone was watching him. When he opened his eyes, he saw an older man with, a head full of white hair, watching him intently. It didn't take long for him to realize this was the man he was looking for. He as an older version of the picture marked Cam and me, he'd found in the envelope his father gave him before he left home.

"I didn't mean to wake you," Cam said.

"I usually don't sleep in the daytime."

"From what I've read, time travel is very tiring. Yes, I believe in that kind of thing. I've been a Trekke for years, just like my grandson Tanner."

"I don't understand."

"I'm sure you don't. Have you ever watched Star Trek?"

He nodded. He'd seen the show while he was at school, but his father would have never allowed him to watch it at home. "I have, but what does that have to do with anything?"

"My daughter says your name is Tony. May I ask your last name?"

"Yes, sir. My last name is Montgomery."

"What is your mother's name?"

"She died of cancer several months ago. Her name was Sherilyn."

"So, she did marry Gerald. Julie says you think I'm your father. If there's anything to this time travel stuff, which I think there is, I could possibly be your father. Can you tell me what you know?"

Tony took a deep breath. "I graduated from college and came home to work for Montgomery Industries. Mom got sick, just before Christmas and we knew she wouldn't last long. She told dad, I mean Gerald, that she wanted me to have my combination Christmas/graduation present while she was still alive to see me get it. They gave me the Land Rover. Six weeks later, we buried her.

"When I got home, about a week ago, I was ordered to leave and never come back. The old man said I could keep the car and he handed me a bankbook. He'd deposited a lot of money to get me out of his life. He told me he'd found a letter, written by my mother, admitting she slept with you and didn't know if you or Gerald was my father.

"I lost everything, my mother, my family and the job I trained for while I was in college. My younger brother, Rick, is going to take over the company and be the son Gerald wanted, rather than the one who he raised. Until that moment, I thought he loved me, but I guess I was mistaken."

"Let me tell you my side of the story," Cam said. "Your mother and I were good friends. I knew about Gerald and how she was planning to marry him. On the night I got my draft notice, one thing led to another and we slept together. She knew I was scared about having to go to Vietnam. It wasn't a certain thing, but I knew, deep in my heart that was where I was going. I wasn't an angel and she wasn't a slut. One thing led to another and I've never regretted that night.

"Three days later I was inducted into the army and after basic training sent to Vietnam, just as I feared. I never heard from your mother again. I decided for her, just like for me, it was one night shared by good friends and nothing more. Oh, I did keep up with her because one of my friends from school told me about her marriage to her father. I was thousands of miles away, but in my thoughts, I wished her well.

"When I came home, I met Julie's mother and we were married. I lost her about three years ago in a car accident. Seeing you, I know you are my son. Whether anyone will ever believe you came here by supernatural means, I can't say, but I do believe such things can and do happen, although they aren't well publicized."

Tony didn't know what to say. Cam Rogers just confirmed everything his father told him. He wondered if he would have been as careless in college if he'd been drafted into military service. He'd always been careful to use condoms when he was with his many girlfriends. With Aids running rampant, he didn't want to take the chance of getting sick. He was positive, he'd never impregnated any of the girls he slept with while at the University of Georgia.

From what he'd learned, things were different in the sixties. He'd read about free love, hippies and draft dodgers. At least Cam Rogers hadn't shirked his duty to his country. More than once, he'd heard how Gerald got out of going into the service because it would have been a hardship for his father. Hardship, hell, Grandpa Montgomery paid some senator a goodly amount of money to get his son deferred. There was no reason Gerald couldn't have served his country, but he got out of it and bragged about it whenever he had a willing audience.

With a minor in history, the Vietnam War always fascinated him. He told himself, he was glad Gerald never had to endure the atrocities perpetuated against the U.S. soldiers as well as the innocent people of that far away country. At least, he felt that way until he listened to what Cam was telling him. He'd gone to fight the battles Gerald Montgomery escaped by having his father buy his way out of the fate of so many young men during the Vietnam years.

~ * ~

"I can't believe Tony is my uncle. How is that possible? He's only a couple of years older than I am."

"You know, that technically he'd not your blood relative," her mother said. "We've always been up front with you about your birth mother. She was my best friend and when she got in trouble, my folks stood by her. Her own parents kicked her out. Your dad and I had just gotten married. We certainly weren't planning a family right away. You were just three days old when she suffered a massive stroke. She lived for about three days. Daddy couldn't stand the thought of her little girl going to strangers. I loved you the minute I saw you. I might not have given birth to you, but you are my daughter in every sense of the word. I made a promise to your mother that I would never allow strangers to take you away.

"As for Tony being my half-brother, by some strange happening, he has been brought here. Perhaps it's a supernatural thing, just like I said earlier. I'm anxious to know more about him. If he is someone who could be special to you, don't let our loyalty to me and your father get in the way of getting to know him. For all intents and purposes, he's all alone in the world."

~ * ~

Although his new found family wanted him to stay with them, he was skeptical. Staying with Jayme and her family would put an imposition onto them. At least that's what his father would have said if they have asked to have a friend stay with them.

"I think I can clear this up," Cam said. "I'm rambling around in that big old house. I can use the company and Tony and I can get better acquainted."

"Whatever you say, Dad. You and Tony will be staying for supper before you leave. I know what you're thinking, but you aren't going to drag him to that greasy spoon you're so fond of. The two of you are going to get a good meal. Besides, Don and Tanner will be here soon and I'm sure they'd like to see you and meet Tony."

"What do you think, son?" Cam asked.

"To be truthful I don't know what to think. Last night I was too tired to go any further, so I pulled over to get some rest. When I went to sleep it was 1990. When I woke up it was 2021. It's just too weird."

"I totally agree," Jayme said. "This is the craziest thing that has ever happened to me. As much as I'd like to have you stay here with us, Grandpa is right. He needs to get to know you better and we do worry about him all alone in town. The way I see it this is the best solution."

"I-I could get a hotel room. I mean for fifty or sixty dollars a night I wouldn't be putting anyone out."

Everyone laughed at his statement. "Now I know you're a time traveler, brother dear," Julie said. "Prices have gone up considerably since 1990. You can't touch a room that's worth staying in for less than a hundred or a hundred and fifty. With this pandemic, it's even worse."

"Pandemic? What's that?"

"It's a long story. Why don't you get cleaned up for supper? Don and Tanner will be here soon. We'll try to explain Covid 19 to you. We'll also have to get you an appointment to get your vaccine."

Everything Julie was telling him was more confusing than enlightening. He decided it was better to let the answers come naturally rather than try to learn everything at once.

~ * ~

"I wish I knew what happened to my family. At least my brother. I guess I don't have a right to call Gerald part of my family," Tony said after supper.

"They don't call me a computer whiz for nothing," Tanner commented. "You don't have to go back town right away do you, Gramps?"

"Of course, not. Why don't you and Tony see what you can find out on the computer while your dad and I check out Tony's Land Rover?"

Tony smiled to himself and handed the keys to Cam. "You can take it for a drive if you want. I think it's a sweet ride."

He could tell both Cam and Don were excited to drive the Land Rover. It would give him some time to see if what Tanner told him was true. According to the younger boy, there wasn't anything that you couldn't find on the Internet.

While Jayme and her mother cleaned up the kitchen, Tanner pulled out what he called a laptop. He remembered the bulky computers he'd used at school but this compact version was beyond his comprehension.

In no time flat, the screen sprung to life. With a few keystrokes, Tanner pulled up what he called a search engine. "What do you want to know first?" he asked.

"I guess I want to know about Gerald. I called him dad for so many years, I wonder if he's still alive."

He watched as Tanner typed in 'Gerald Montgomery'. Amazingly several sites popped up. For some reason, he was saddened when he saw that Gerald died of a stroke in 1999. He'd been gone for twenty-two years, years that Tony missed entirely when he traveled through time.

Under Gerald's name, he saw a listing for Montgomery Industries. When Tanner clicked on it, the information was amazing.

Do to failing health, Gerald Montgomery sold the company in 1996. With no heirs to carry on the business, it was purchased by Dresden Chemical but went bankrupt in 2007.

Tony swallowed down the tears that threatened to flow at any minute. Montgomery Industries was supposed to be his future. Not only had he lost thirty-one years but what he thought was going to be his no longer existed.

"Anything else you want to research?" Tanner asked.

"What happened to my little brother, Rick?"

Again, Tanner's fingers flew across the keys. As had happened before a lengthy list of sites came up.

Richard (Rick) Montgomery is best known for being crowned Miss Gay Las Vegas in 2001. Under the name of Sophie Mars, he has been performing in Las Vegas as a female impersonator since 1996. He and his husband, Greg Turney, own an estate in Las Vegas as well as a vacation home in Cabo, Mexico.

"How can that be?" he questioned.

"What do you mean?"

"How can two men be married?"

"That's easy. Same sex marriage has been legal for many years. A lot of same sex couples adopt children. The way this reads your brother is a celebrity. It doesn't surprise me that he and his partner haven't adopted children. Being a performer, children would be a determent to say nothing of a target for the press. I'll scroll down and see if I can find a picture."

After scrolling through the information, a picture of a beautiful woman dominated the screen. Even with the makeup, he could see Rick in the woman's eyes. "Th-that's my brother? Damn I knew he liked men, but I certainly never thought he'd do anything like this. Is there any way I can contact him?"

"Let me do some research. I'll come into town tomorrow and let you know what I find out. Most of those guys are hard to get in touch with. They seem to like their privacy, or so I've read."

Tony agreed. He'd learned more than he thought possible about both the man he called dad for most of his life and the brother he'd loved ever since he was born. Would Rick even believe he was his brother?

"Any chance I can get you to leave your vehicle out here for a while?" Don asked, when he came into the living room. "I know Pops doesn't have enough garage space for it. That said, a vehicle in this condition would be too tempting sitting on the street."

"You're kidding, right?"

"No, I'm not. There have been several car thefts in the area recently. Since the pandemic first started, people have been desperate for money. Considering your insurance probably lapsed at least thirty years ago, it will be safe in my shop under lock and key. Tomorrow I'll come into town and we can get it insured as well as registered. You go driving it on the highway, and you'd be picked up for numerous ticket able offenses."

"Why would anyone want to steal my car?"

"It's simple. It's in pristine condition, low milage and a collector's item. Believe me I know cars and this one is worth a bundle. If you want to sell it and get something newer, I'd be willing to find a buyer for it. That's what I do for a living."

"I agree with Don," Cam said. "Besides, your driver's license is out of date. We need to remedy that. Anyway, it's getting dark. I'd just as soon be home before it gets much later."

As much as Tony wanted to stay and talk to Tanner about the all the things he could find out on the Internet, he also knew he needed to get some sleep. The cat nap he'd taken earlier had taken the edge off his exhaustion, but it was coming back.

Also by the Author
at
Rogue Phoenix Press

Awake in a New World
The New World Book One

Caroline Lewis feels life isn't worth living when she loses her husband to Covid-19 while on a business trip to China. In order to avoid the coming pandemic, she opts to have her body frozen to be awakened in 2070. In 2120, archaeologists exploring the ruins of Los Angeles find Caroline's perfectly preserved body. As she is brought to life, fifty years later than expected, she is forced to learn to live in a world unlike the one she remembers from 2020. Aaron Phillips knows Caroline is special when he hires her as a research volunteer at the library. He hopes she feels the same way about him.

Unwanted in a New World
The New World Book Two

Orphaned at birth, Christopher is sent to a ranch for unwanted children. When he ages out, he is embraced by a militant group of skinheads who are unaware of his Native American heritage. A protest at an Alien Complex outside of Denver opens a new path for his life. While he is receiving his education, his new friends and mentors are working behind the scene to find his birth family.

Melian has come to the complex from the Alien base under the Antarctic ice cap. She takes an immediate interest in Christopher, who now wants to be called Chris, and looks forward to see what their future holds.

Alone in a New World
The New World Book Three

As a child of four, Marco is all alone in the world. With only his mother in his life, her death prompts the authorities to send him to Henderson Ranch for boys. At the age of eighteen, he is sold into slavery to a ranch in Mexico. Two years later, he is recued and reunited with his childhood friend, Christopher. At his friend's insistence he modernizes his name to Mark and embarks on a journey that will bring him full circle back to Henderson Ranch, now called Resurrection Ranch. On his journey, Mark finds previously unknown family and love with one of the alien nurses, Kara, all of whom are willing to journey with him into the future at Resurrection Ranch.

Lost and Found in a New World
The New World Book Four

Peter was kidnapped by his father and sold to Henderson Ranch. There he worked without an education, until his eighteenth birthday when he was sold as a slave to a ranch in Mexico. Once he was rescued, he reunited with some of the others he'd known at Henderson Ranch as well as the mother he'd never forgotten. Helping his friends, Chris and Mark, he becomes involved in the rebuilding of the ranch where they grew up, renaming it Resurrection Ranch, where others like themselves, can work and be given the education they were deprived as children. Before leaving for the ranch, he meets Jerilyn, a therapist who will be transferring to Resurrection Ranch. Almost instantly, he knows she is someone he wants in his life.

The Return of the Ancients
The Aliens Book One

Nina is devastated when she realizes she must leave Plantas along with the man who is to become her mate, Ragnar, and her best friend, Tarena. When Nina arrives on Earth in Peru at the Nazca plains, she is greeted by a young archaeology student, Rand Jacobson. Even though she is attracted to Rand, she is still grieving the loss of Ragnar.

Ragnar is surprised when, after being greeted as a god on the planet Seros, the military opens fire on his family. After being taken prisoner, he is treated like a lab rat until a scientist, Geni, comes to his rescue. At her estate, he learns the physicians who work with her have saved the lives of his family and friends.

My Uncle the King
The Aliens Book Two

When three contingencies took off from their dying planet, Plantas, only two arrived at their destination unharmed. When the lost contingency is hit with a meteor storm, only one ship survives and makes it to their destination of Nalo. Over the generations, the descendants of the original refugees become the ruling class of their adopted planet. Even the rebel group, the Pure Of Nalo, are unable to unseat the monarchy. When relations with Earth are established, it is Prince Nicos who leaves Nalo to find love on an alien planet and bring back new ideas as well as his Earthly family to save the throne and the people of Nalo.

You Again

While attending college at the University of Wisconsin in the 1960s, Carole Martinson fell in love and eloped with Phillip Vanderlin. When his parents realized she was a farmer's daughter and below them socially, they insisted they divorce.

Fast forward to 2019 and Carole is invited to a wedding cruise financed by her granddaughter's fiancé's grandfather. With no knowledge about the groom's family, Carole flies to Florida for the cruise she and her second husband never got to take. Upon her arrival, she immediately recognizes Phillip.

Phillip never forgot his first love. He is thrilled when he realizes the grandmother is the girl he was forced to leave behind so many years ago.

About the Author

Sherry Derr-Wille began her writing career in her sophomore English class in high school. Challenged to get an A on the first test, she won the right to sit in the back of the room and write for a year. At the end of the year no one told her to stop the assignment, so she didn't. At her 40th class reunion, she realized she was the only one who enjoyed the assignment. It was too late because by that time she'd signed seventeen contracts for her work.

Wife to her high school sweetheart of over fifty years, she is the mother of three, grandmother of nine and great-grandmother of six. She is retired and lives in a mid-sized town close to the Illinois border in Southern Wisconsin. Her mantra is READ LOCAL AND BE TRANSPORTED TO ANOTHER WORLD.

VISIT OUR WEBSITE
FOR THE FULL INVENTORY
OF QUALITY BOOKS:

http://www.roguephoenixpress.com

Rogue Phoenix Press

Representing Excellence in Publishing

Quality trade paperbacks and downloads
in multiple formats,
in genres ranging from historical to contemporary romance,
mystery and science fiction.
Visit the website then bookmark it.
We add new titles each month!

www.ingramcontent.com/pod-product-compliance
Lightning Source LLC
Chambersburg PA
CBHW051952220626
47052CB00004B/909